Dead Man at Snake's Creek

Credence, Texas, is a one-horse town. Dying on its feet since the closure of the Shawnee Trail, the place is divided by bitterness, resentment and feuds that have smouldered on for years.

This is what Johnny Hartford finds when he returns home for his brother's wedding. Ten years before, he left the town in a blaze of glory to travel to Chicago to become a Pinkerton Agent. But that was before the war. Now everything has changed: his dying father will barely speak to him, his brother is running wild and longhorn rustling is rife. Determined to make amends with his family and catch the cattle thieves, Hartford turns to old Sheriff Milton for help. But the day after he arrives, a prominent local rancher is shot in the back and Hartford discovers that almost everyone in the town has a reason for wanting him dead.

Dead Man at Snake's Creek

Rob Hill

A Black Horse Western

ROBERT HALE

© Rob Hill 2017
First published in Great Britain 2017

ISBN 978-0-7198-2576-7

The Crowood Press
The Stable Block
Crowood Lane
Ramsbury
Marlborough
Wiltshire SN8 2HR

www.bhwesterns.com

Robert Hale is an imprint
of The Crowood Press

Typeset by
Derek Doyle & Associates, Shaw Heath
Printed and bound in Great Britain by
CPI Group (UK) Ltd, Croydon, CR0 4YY

For Val

INTRODUCTION

The moment the shot echoed against the limestone walls of Snake's Creek, startled vermilion flycatchers erupted upwards from the cypresses along the river like sparks out of a wood fire. The cicadas were shocked into silence. The hot afternoon air was still. Even the river gurgling over its stony bed seemed to pause. The rider who had just turned his horse back along the riverside track swayed in his saddle. As he toppled sideways, the reins slipped from his hands, his feet flipped themselves out of his stirrups and he crashed down into the reeds at the water's edge.

The back of the man's jacket was as torn and bloody as if he had been flayed and a dark red stain soiled the front of his shirt. His eyes were open, cold blue and stared at nothing. His cheeks were clean-shaven and his sideburns were grey. But the moment after he had been shot his face showed only empty surprise. There was no expression to suggest what kind of man he had been. Kind or cruel? Generous or mean? Loving or hateful? He had died rich though. His jacket was well cut, his silk vest was embroidered and his boots were new. He wore a gold signet ring on his finger, embossed with a letter D in italic script, and on his hip was a .45 in a tooled leather holster.

The dead man's horse was at a loss. She stood over him for a while, then leaned down and nuzzled him as if she was trying to wake him up. A well-groomed mare, her glossy black coat shone like silk. Her ears pointed forward, stiff and sharp. She knew.

Then another man hurried along the path, running awkwardly, short of breath. He knelt down beside the body and stared at the pale face. His hand shook as he rested his fingers on the neck to be certain there was no pulse. It only took a second. A trickle of blood had emerged from the side of the mouth. He brushed his palm over the eyelids and pushed himself to his feet.

Grabbing the reins of the mare, he pulled her away and slapped her rump to send her home. Then he retrieved a fishing pole that had got lodged in the reeds and made his way back along the path to where the others were waiting.

ONE

The previous day

At eight in the morning, the heat which would soon dominate the day was already bending the prairie air. The far horizon was corrugated, liquid almost, and a primrose sun burst against the pale sky. From the top of a rise, a lone rider paused to take in the view of Credence, the little cottonwood town down on the empty plain, built as a stopover for riders on the Shawnee Trail in the years before the war.

The rider's hat was pulled down low and his jacket and pants were coated in white caliche dust. Square-shouldered and sparely built, he sat tall in the saddle. He ignored the rivulets of sweat on his cheeks and the taste of dust on his lips. His chiselled face had a stoic look as if he was used to shrugging off hardship and as he stared out across the landscape, his gaze was unflinching. His thoughts raced, though – he hadn't been home for ten years and didn't anticipate an easy reception. As he sat there, he unfastened the

9

steel badge from the front of his jacket and carefully pinned it out of sight on the inside.

Reaching down to unhitch his canteen, he instinctively leaned forward, gently patted the neck of his horse, a fine appaloosa, and whispered some encouragement in her ear. The horse nickered affectionately in reply. Clearly, the two of them had shared this conversation many times before.

An hour later, the rider made his way up the town's main street. The sun-bleached storefronts had seen better days; the blistered paintwork had gone unretouched, shingles were missing from roofs, and the hitching rail outside the grocery had come off its posts and lay in the dirt. The door to the sheriff's office was closed against the heat. There was no one about.

As the rider approached the saloon, an old timer who had been dozing in a wicker chair on the porch was jolted awake by the sound of the approaching hoof beats. He jumped up, screwed his eyes tight to try to make out who was coming then scuttled inside. Red and white paper streamers were looped along the porch rail between bright home-made rosettes. Above the door hung a faded old sign which proclaimed 'Pearl of the West'.

Stepping in from the harsh sunlight, the rider stood in the doorway and waited for his eyes to accustom to the shadows.

'Well, look who it ain't.' A woman's voice singsonged out to him. 'Johnny Hartford home at last. Thought you'd left us for good.'

The saloon was a barn of a place built to hold a hundred drinkers and card players and still have room to spare. A thin carpet of trail dust lay inside the door. Wooden tables and chairs, which had been repaired and re-repaired, lined the walls and between the roof beams someone had looped more paper streamers. High in the pitch of the roof some shingles must have shifted as lines of bright sunlight fell through and allowed golden dust motes to spiral like fireflies. Above the bar, which was also draped with bunting and rosettes, hung the saloon clock and a pair of mighty longhorns, a reminder of better days.

Hartford's eyes settled on the woman at the bar. Obviously delighted to see him, her eyes sparkled. Her long dark hair was tied back and she wore a man's work shirt with the sleeves rolled up, pants and boots. Thirty years old maybe, there was shrewd intelligence in her face. A twelve-gauge scattergun rested across her knees.

'Pearl . . .' Hartford began, but before he could continue, the woman interrupted.

'Gun at the door, Hart.' This time her voice was firm. 'Peg's right there.'

Hartford was about to say something but noticed the woman's hand move towards the twelve-gauge. He shrugged and started to unbuckle his gun belt. There were two Colts in their belts already hanging there.

As his hands went to his gun belt, nobody spoke. The old timer who had perched himself on a bar stool beside Pearl stared at him; a man sitting alone at a table looked up from his solitaire game; two trail hands at a table with a bottle and a deck of cards between them turned towards him. When Hartford hung his gun beside the others, everyone in the room breathed. The men went back to their cards, the old timer edged round Hartford on his way to his chair on the porch, Pearl put the shotgun down on the bar and beckoned Hartford over to a corner table.

'Back for the wedding?'

The question was innocent enough, but Hartford heard concern in her voice.

'Ain't every day your brother gets hitched,' Hartford said.

'Doing the right thing like always.' Pearl looked him in the eye. 'You just tread careful now you're back here, then you won't step on nobody's toes.'

'You never used to keep a scattergun in here.' Hart was aware that everyone in the room was listening.

'Trouble a few weeks back. Didn't amount to much.' Pearl didn't want to be drawn and changed tack. 'They plan on holding the wedding breakfast here – not that your brother's come up with the down payment he promised.'

She indicated the bunting.

'Looks good.' Hartford glanced round at the decorations. 'You got any rooms free?'

'Not heading out to your pa's place?' Pearl studied his face. 'It's Friday morning now, wedding ain't till one o'clock Sunday. That should give you plenty of time to make up.'

'I jus' . . .' Hartford hesitated. 'Don't reckon I'll be staying out there, that's all.'

'Got all the rooms you want.' Pearl didn't ask him to explain. 'Can't remember when we last had a visitor. Surprised you've come back, that's all.'

Hartford waited for her to go on.

'Shawnee Trail's dead and buried. Town's a shadow of what it was when my pa opened this place.'

Hart remembered a time when the saloon had been crowded with cowboys with pay in their pockets on their way back from Missouri. But the Shawnee only lasted for a single season after the war ended, four years ago now. Missouri farmers claimed the longhorns brought fever that infected their herds. Angry vigilantes set up blockades and a local law was passed to prevent Texas beeves from crossing the state line. Since then, drives from this part of Texas headed up the Chisolm Trail to the new railhead at Abilene.

'If I could find a buyer, I'd sell this place and move to Dallas.' Pearl cast her eye round the saloon. Apart from the whisper of cards being dealt, the place was silent. 'Usually I just got Pops Wardell and Bill Greely in here. Pops is the old guy out on the porch.'

Greely looked up from his solitaire hand when he heard his name. His face was thin, with pasty, blood-hound features. A three-day growth of grey stubble clung to his cheeks. Being tall, he was used to stooping so as not to draw attention to himself and, even sitting at a table, his narrow shoulders seemed to

13

hunch over his cards.

'I run the livery, if you need your horse taking care of.' His friendly smile showed blackened teeth.

'The other two,' Pearl lowered her voice and indicated the trail hands on the other side of the saloon. 'They're here because they just got fired from the Lazy D.'

'Dunmore's place?' Hart said.

'Someone's been cutting the herd. They caught one guy and he's in jail.

'Dunmore accused these two but didn't have any proof, so he fired them anyway.'

The two men didn't look up from their poker game. Hartford couldn't tell whether they had heard. Pearl lowered her voice to a whisper.

'You've got to be careful.' She hesitated. 'I'm telling you, Hart. Dunmore is used to getting what he wants. He ain't at all keen on this wedding and you know what a hothead your brother is.'

Pearl searched his face. Had he heeded her warning?

'Talking about that son-of-a-bitch Dunmore?' One of the trail hands put down his cards and called across to Pearl.

His dark eyes were stone-hard and a raspberry-coloured blush worked its way up his neck at the mention of the name of his old boss. He was clean-shaven with a clipped moustache, powerfully built with strong arms and shoulders. He wore a black Stetson hat, which he kept brushed free of trail dust, and his shirt was pressed, the collar folded and the cuffs buttoned. A small moustache comb peeped out of the pocket of his shirt. He knew that taking pride in his appearance set him apart from the other ranch hands.

'We've worked three seasons out at the Lazy D and he comes up with all kinds of accusations, calls in the sheriff and we end up fired.' As he spoke, he balled his hands into fists. 'Accused us without a spit of proof. Sheriff takes his word and slings Jake Nudd in jail just because he couldn't remember where he was the night a few head went missing.'

The man was angry and he didn't care who heard. His lips were tight as if his words tasted sour.

'What Logan says is right. Dunmore wouldn't even listen to us.' The second man, Clyde Shorter, spoke up in support of his friend and placed his cards down on the table in exactly the same way, as if he was copying him.

Heavily built for a cowboy, he was older than Logan, with thin hair and the wisp of a beard over doughy cheeks. His voice was high and nasal-sounding, a whine to Logan's drawl. Logan speaking out first gave him the confidence to chime in. He wanted Logan to know that he was backing him up.

'I've drove chuck wagons back and forth to Missouri for years,' he added indignantly. 'Never been treated like this.'

'One day somebody's going to put a bullet in Dunmore.' Logan glared contemptuously at his friend. 'Might just be me.'

'Another thing is,' the second man wanted to

make sure he impressed Logan. 'He ain't even paid us what he owes. We've worked three weeks this month, lived out there in that rat hole bunkhouse in this heat and then he fires us.' He searched for a way of showing Logan just how profound his resentment was. 'Only let me buy the worst beans, the ones that stay hard even when you soak 'em for days. One time there was so many weevils in the flour sacks he gave me, damn things practically walked along by themselves. Point is who do the men blame when they get gut ache? Me, ain't it?' The man shook his head. 'Dunmore's got Tom McInnon's boy doing the cooking now, sixteen years old and never rustled up a plate of chow in his life. Kicks me out and replaces me with a kid. If Logan ain't the one to put a bullet in Dunmore, then it'll be me.'

Clyde Shorter made sure he caught Logan's eye.

'Overheard what you've been saying.' Pops Wardell stood in the doorway, eager to put in his two cents worth. 'Dunmore threw me off his land last year. I was up at Snake's Creek. They've got shovel heads and fork tails up there, fat ones.

'Been fishing there since I don't know when. Used to go up there with your pa until he took sick.' Pops looked to Hartford hoping he would back him up. Hartford nodded politely. 'Anyhow, there I was with my pole and along comes Dunmore, all high and mighty, and tells me to get the hell off his land.'

Logan picked up his cards and studied them. Clyde Shorter did the same.

'Told him I'd been coming up there for years, but

it didn't make no difference. Still said I had to get the hell out. Said he didn't want anyone up there on account of rustlers. What kind of rustling did he think I was doing with a fishing pole?' Pops laughed and waited for the others to share his joke.

Logan ignored him and gestured with his cards to show that the game should begin again.

'I'd put a bullet in him, yes sir.' Pops made one more bid for recognition by the others. He wanted to show Logan that he had a beef with Dunmore too. When no one took any notice of him, he fell back on repetition and hollow threats. 'Been going up there since I don't know when and he treats me like that. If he thinks he's going to stop me fishing out at Snake's, he's got another think coming.'

'Hardly the same, is it?' Logan didn't look up from his cards. 'Jake Nudd is locked in a jail cell, me and Clyde get canned and you're worried about going fishing.'

Pops fell silent, trying to think of a way of getting back to his chair on the porch without losing face or aggravating Logan further.

'Did you catch any, Pops?' Pearl came to his rescue.

'Yeah, flathead catfish.' Pops held his hands apart to show how big.

'Tell you one thing.' Not wanting to be left out, Greely looked up from his solitaire. 'Dunmore is the only rancher round here who never gives me a tip. I take care of his horse every time he comes into town.'

'Heard you say that before.' Pops offered his

support to Greely as he turned and headed out to the porch again. 'Never come across anyone so mean. One of these days Dunmore will get what's coming. You mark my words.'

Pearl had had enough of listening to the men griping. She stood up.

'Room overlooks the street.' She turned to Hartford. 'I'll find you a blanket. It gets cold at night.'

Hartford left the men to their cards and followed Pearl up the wooden stairs. The room contained a brass bedstead with a horsehair mattress, a marble-topped washstand holding a china bowl and jug, and a wooden chair. Everything was covered in a fine layer of dust.

'Thanks.' Hartford's boot heels clacked on the bare boards. 'Weeks since I slept in a bed.'

'I sold the sheets.' Pearl came in holding a blanket and a thin pillow. 'Trader came through and made me an offer. No one stays here now, so I thought why not.'

Hartford looked out of the window at the empty street. Bill Greely was leading his horse past the sheriff's office on the way to the livery.

'Old Henry Milton still sheriff?'

'Sure is.' Pearl laughed fondly. 'Just about to retire though. Place won't be the same without him. Did you know he arrived on the same wagon train as my ma and pa?'

Hartford smiled; he had heard the story often enough. Milton and Pearl's family were some of the first settlers in this part of the county. Pearl had been born here. Milton had taken charge of law and order while her pa built the saloon with his own hands and named it after his baby daughter on the day she was born.

'Old Henry knows every stick and stone in the place, all the people too, inside and out. Kind of glues the place together, what's left of it.'

'Never thought he'd retire,' Hartford said.

'Arthritis in his knees. Can't hardly climb up into the saddle now.' Pearl put the blanket down on the bed. There was something she had to know. 'Does your pa know you're back for the wedding?'

'Nope.' Hartford continued staring out of the window. Greely had almost reached the end of the street. 'I know. You're going to tell me to be careful.'

'He's sick, Hart. Been sick a long time. It's good that you'll see him, even if you ain't exactly welcome.'

'Him and my brother, Boone, I don't expect either of them will be pleased to see me.'

'Best get out to the farm then. Catch your pa on his own. Boone ain't there right now.'

'No?' Hartford turned to her.

'He's taken a job in Dallas. There's so much building going on, they're taking on guys from all over. Pay good money too.'

'Who's looking after the farm?' Hartford was taken aback.

'Your sister, Annie. Who else?' Pearl stared at him trying to gauge his reaction. 'Boone's fiancée, Mary

May Dunmore, keeps her company out there. Boone comes back when he can, at least that's what he says. You can imagine what old man Dunmore thinks of that.'

Hartford looked for Greely out in the street but he was gone.

'You've been away a long time, Hart.'

TWO

The farm where Hartford grew up was five miles south of town. After he had eaten the plate of eggs and cornbread Pearl made for him, he let her persuade him that he should head out there without delay. She insisted that even if Hartford couldn't make peace with his pa, at least the sick man wouldn't hear about his son's presence in the area from someone else.

Pearl was right, ten years was a long time. Hartford realized that there was good chance that she was close to guessing the real reason why he had suddenly turned up back in his home town. She hadn't asked him a single question about Chicago, what he had done in the war or how he had spent his time since. She would have remembered the local reaction when he had been due to leave just as clearly as he did. She would have heard the gossip about what Joe Hartford's boy was doing up north and would certainly have heard the rumours about his war

21

service. She would know that his father had forbidden him to set foot in his house ever again. Hartford could imagine his sister, Annie, with no one to talk to out on the isolated farm except her ill, widowed pa, riding in to town to confide in her.

The morning sun climbed the china sky and a few threads of cloud stretched high overhead. Along the trail, saguaro cactus flowers were bunched as tight as fists against the daylight and the smell of sagebrush was overpowering. In the distance, the shimmering air fractured the line of the horizon. Hartford smiled at the sight of a family of jack rabbits, which bounced ahead of him for a while before veering off the track to take cover behind the safety of a bunch of turkey foot.

The heat burned Hartford's shoulders as he let the appaloosa amble along. Was he deliberately letting his horse walk slowly? With the farm so close, he was aware of a sick feeling lying in his gut. For years, he had known this day would come, the day he attempted to make peace with his pa. Annie's letters had kept him in touch with the course of his father's illness, his decline from the strong, fit guy who had arrived in this part of Texas with his young wife, staked his claim, created a farm out of untamed land and built a house for his family with his own two hands. Now Pa Hartford contemptuously referred to himself as a lunger. He was a shadow of the man he had been, emaciated and bitter-tempered. His wife had worked herself to death and now TB sat like an anvil on his chest. He had to fight for every breath, barely able to summon the strength to raise himself out of the chair on the porch where he spent his days to stumble indoors to the couch where he spent his nights. In spite of this, he had forbidden Hartford, the son for whom he had had the highest hopes, from ever returning home again.

Annie's letters were quite clear that his pa had not changed his mind nor was he ever likely to. But Hartford had to come; he had to try. Since their mother died, he was well aware of how hard Annie worked, taking care of Pa, the house, farm chores and dealing with Boone's excitable nature, even though Annie's letters never referred to her own struggles. They were full of Pa's illness and the domestic ups and downs of living with Boone. Although recently, after passing on the news about Boone's engagement to Mary May Dunmore, Annie had barely mentioned him. Hartford judged there was a lot she wasn't telling him.

Another mile, Hartford knew he would be able to see the farm. Up ahead from a ridge where he and Boone used to trap rabbits when they were boys, there was a view over the whole spread. He remembered watching his pa in the far distance out mending fences or herding his few sheep and once observing him and men he had hired from the town raise the barn. At the time, this simple construction seemed to him like a miracle that promised hope and prosperity. As Hartford thought about these things, he was aware of the sick feeling returning to the pit of his stomach.

The news Pearl had given him didn't add up. Boone working on a construction site in Dallas, Annie running the farm, Boone's fiancée keeping Annie company and old man Dunmore furious about his daughter's engagement to his good-for-nothing neighbour, a sodbuster's son. Then there was his desperately sick pa, too stubborn to let bygones be bygones. Only Annie would be pleased to see him. Boone and his pa held him in various degrees of contempt. Hartford reined in the appaloosa, unhitched the canteen which Pearl had filled for him and unscrewed the cap. The fresh water tasted honey-sweet and ran cool down his throat.

Once Hartford had replaced the canteen, his hand instinctively slipped inside his jacket to check for his badge. If his pa hadn't been sick, then, yes, he would have worn it for all to see. But even though it was the single thing in his life of which he was most proud, he knew it would get his pa riled like nothing else. Now was not the time to draw attention. The badge Hartford was so proud of was a silver shield embossed with the words Pinkerton National Detective Agency.

When Hartford was a teenager, his mother read a profile of Alan Pinkerton in an out-of-date copy of *Harper's Weekly* she bought from an itinerant trader. Pinkerton was a Scots immigrant whose North Western Police Agency had established a reputation for integrity and fairness. He was just about to start a new Detective Company under his own name headquartered at number 80 Washington Street, Chicago.

Having struggled to maintain her own high standards for years whilst living amongst the ill-educated ranch hands, cowpokes and drifters who came and went on her husband's farm, Rose Hartford wanted something better for her sons.

Rose loved her husband and, true to her marriage vows, would have followed him anywhere, but the way of life he had chosen for them had worn her out. Pinkerton's crusading zeal, as it was reported in the article, made a deep impression on her. For one thing it reminded her of her own father, also a Scot, a Presbyterian minister of iron-clad convictions, who had set sail for the New World with the intention of creating a better life for his family and spreading the Word of the Lord.

Tragically, the bronchitis Rose's father contracted on the voyage from Liverpool turned to pneumonia and he died before the ship docked in New York. Within a few months, Rose accepted an offer of marriage from Joe Hartford, an honest, hardworking man who had made up his mind to travel to Texas, establish his own small farm and raise a family.

Years later when Rose read the *Harper's Weekly* description of The Pinkerton Code, it reminded her of her beloved father's idealism. She read and reread it: accept no bribes, never compromise with criminals, turn down reward money, refuse cases that could initiate a scandal. It was like music to her. It was obvious that her younger son, Johnny, should be the one to make the long journey to Chicago, seek out Mr Pinkerton and offer his services. Johnny was the quiet one: intelligent, thoughtful and strong. She saw her own father's upright nature in him. This was the way in which at least one of her sons could create a better life for himself, far removed from the daily grind of the farm. Anyway, the farm was too small to support all five of them now the boys and Annie were grown up, so her husband would be bound to agree.

Her elder son, Boone, was erratic. Wild and handsome so that he caught the eye of the girls in town, she suspected his reckless nature made the boys his age secretly afraid of him. Boone resented his chores on the farm and argued with his father. He got into fights in town and on more than one occasion Sheriff Milton had brought him home.

Rose Hartford made the case to her husband that, with Johnny gone, Boone would see the farm as his birthright, settle down and work hard. Joe Hartford agreed. Although he barely shared her confidence in Boone, he could see that farm could not support all five of them. Secretly he had always hoped that Annie would be the one to go. Married to a local rancher, he hoped she might bring a modest dowry in the form of some discount on a livestock purchase or at least a deal over winter feed. But Joe knew better than to incur his wife's wrath by mentioning this, so he kept quiet and agreed that Johnny should make the trek to Chicago and join the Pinkertons.

Johnny Hartford was nineteen. His quiet determination and clear sense of right and wrong were immediately obvious to Allan Pinkerton. In addition, Pinkerton was deeply impressed by the fact that

Hartford had travelled all the way from Texas to join his new agency. He took him on. Hartford found cheap lodgings round the corner from the Washington Street office and went to work. His enthusiastic letters home described exciting assignments guarding freight shipments on the new mid-west rail network. His mother was thrilled because it was clear to her that her precious son was doing good in the world. His father basked in reflected glory and took the opportunity to regale anyone in town who would listen with the contents of the latest letter. Annie was excited. Boone was jealous.

One Christmas, a letter arrived on Agency notepaper which bore the legend 'We Never Sleep' underneath an etching of a wide open human eye. Rose, Annie and Joe had never seen an image so dramatic. The notion that they had a direct personal contact with a member of the Pinkerton Agency dazed them with pride; they could hardly speak. There was even more thrilling news to come.

In February, their Johnny, in the company of Alan Pinkerton himself, was assigned to protect President-elect Lincoln on a rail journey to Washington when a plot to sabotage the track and derail the train as it passed through Baltimore was uncovered. Members of the agency, including Hartford, worked up a plan which involved Lincoln switching trains, passing through Baltimore at night and cutting telegraph wires to ensure that the plotters were not able to communicate. When Rose and Joe received details of this in their next letter, they were beyond excitement. Their younger son, their Johnny, was a national hero.

But in their small Texas cattle town, the reaction to Johnny Hartford's latest exploits was muted. Political tension was mounting across the country and President-elect Lincoln wasn't popular down here. Neighbours who had previously listened keenly to the Hartfords' news turned away. The townsfolk they had known for years listened politely to Joe and Rose, but eyebrows were raised. So Lincoln had slipped away under cover of darkness? In their eyes, that branded the President-elect a coward. Later, when no assassins were actually arrested, let alone charged, they didn't know what to believe.

Then the war came and everything changed. Johnny Hartford had joined the Pinkerton Agency eighteen months before the outbreak. To his parents, it was perfectly logical for him to continue working for them while the politicians got things sorted out. But as the months passed, the conflict snowballed and the enormity of what was about to happen became clear, they could not help wanting their son back home.

At this point, neither Joe, Rose nor Annie had heard from Johnny for months. No mail could get through, so they pretended to themselves he was still guarding freight out of Chicago. But they heard the rumours: Allan Pinkerton's agency was supplying secret intelligence for General McClellan's Army of the Potomac; Pinkerton agents infiltrated groups of

Southern sympathisers in the north; they had even set up spy rings behind enemy lines here in the South.

By this time most of the local men were away fighting. When Rose made one of her trips to the store, she was shunned by the other women. They were used to Rose proudly passing on news about Johnny, but now they were worried sick about their husbands and sons, with danger in the air and all the rumours flying around, it was too much for them to take. For months, they had put up with being reminded that Rose's beloved Johnny, who, unlike their own men folk, was too good for farm work, was making a success of his life beyond anything they could ever hope for their own children. But now, as news of the first casualties filtered back to Credence, rumours about Johnny Hartford ripped through the little town like wildfire: he had been overheard in a saloon in Abilene trying to buy dynamite for heaven knows what purpose; he had masterminded a spy-ring which had led to the deaths of good Southern men; he had been captured and was being held in Andersonville waiting to be shot as a spy.

Boone also heard these rumours. To the approval of the townsfolk, he declared grandly that he was leaving to join the Texas Brigade under General Hood. The hired hands had already been seduced by the recruiting sergeant's promise of adventure and army pay months ago. Alone on the farm with his wife and daughter, the recruiters' dire warnings rang in Joe Hartford's ears: if he failed to join up, the

29

Yankees would ride in one day, kill him, slit his wife and daughter's throats, steal his farm and there would be nothing he could do about it. They also promised him regular pay which he could send home. Joe Hartford left his scattergun with Rose and joined.

The good news was that, unlike so many of their neighbours, both Joe and Boone survived the war. Boone was wounded at Gaines' Mill, which allowed him home leave, but somehow the wound didn't heal so he never made it back to the line. Joe, having endured the horrors of Manassas and Sharpsburg, was taken prisoner after Devil's Den and spent the rest of the war in Elmira Prison in New York where the death rate due to hunger and disease was as bad as any battlefield. If it hadn't been for his skill in catching prison rats, he would have starved.

While the men were away, Rose died. Worn out by work and worry, with a meagre diet and ostracised by her neighbours, she only had Annie to rely on. The farm fell to rack and ruin. Broken fences remained unrepaired because the storekeeper's wife refused to sell them any wire; one night, someone stole all their sheep; neglected longhorns from a neighbouring ranch got in and trampled their vegetable patch. The one thing that would have sustained Rose through all this misery would have been a letter from Johnny. It did not come.

On her own, Annie was powerless to prevent her mother's decline. When Rose died, Annie was unwilling to risk asking anyone in the town for help, dug the grave herself and read the twenty-third psalm, Rose's favourite, over the body. She then lived in the house with the chickens to make sure they couldn't wander off, slept with the shotgun Joe had left behind in her bed and waited for the men to return.

Hartford dismounted when his horse reached the top of the ridge. Far below, a handkerchief of irrigated land stood out emerald green against the surrounding scrub. From here it looked as though the house, the old barn and the fences were all in a decent state of repair. There was an extensive vegetable patch and he could see rows of melons and potatoes lining the bank of the stream that ran through the property, the reason Joe had settled here in the first place. A single goat was tethered further down the bank where his pa had once let sheep graze and a hen house still stood in the yard. Hartford smiled to himself at the sight of the old place. He half expected to catch sight of his ma weeding between the rows of vegetables, while his brother Boone set up a row of tin cans on the fence to knock down with his catapult. South of the farm lay mile after mile of open plain. In the distance, a dust cloud kicked up by a herd of longhorns hung in the air. The Hartfords' immediate neighbour was the Lazy D ranch.

After he had spent a few minutes taking in the view, Hartford made his way down the slope to the farm. The heat on the south side of the ridge was more intense. It burned his shoulders and the sunlight bounced off the prairie floor, almost blinding him. His heartbeat quickened as he approached the farm, but he kept the appaloosa at the same measured walking place.

There was someone sitting in a rocking chair on the porch. Asleep, Hartford assumed. But as he drew closer, the man reached down beside him and picked up a scattergun, heaved himself out of his chair and took up a position leaning against one of the porch posts. He raised the gun to his shoulder, pointed it straight at Hartford and called out.

'Stop right there.'

THREE

'Who are you?' Joe Hartford kept his aim steady.

Dressed in clean work clothes, his shirt hung loose over his narrow shoulders where he had lost weight, his face was pain-lined and pale. Leaning heavily against the porch post while he pointed the shotgun at Hartford's chest, he looked as though he was set on defending his property to his last breath.

'It's me, Pa.'

Joe stared at his son as he would at any stranger who unexpectedly turned up, reluctant to trust him without proof of his good intentions.

From inside the house, came the sound of men arguing. Hartford couldn't make out what they were saying but one of them sounded older, angrier. The force of his voice showed that he was used to being in command. The younger man's voice was whiney, a spoiled kid wanting his own way. Even from out here you could hear the stamp of boot heels on the bare floorboards as one of them paced up and down.

On the far side of the yard, Hartford recognized

33

the old family buggy, battered but still serviceable, although its leather seats were split in places and some of the wooden spokes were repaired with wire binding. In front of the house, a groomed black mare was tied to the porch rail. It carried a saddle with a polished bone horn and expensively tooled leather skirts and obviously belonged to one of the men inside. The older man, Hartford decided. At the sound of his master's raised voice, the horse pulled against his tether as if he was afraid.

'Pa,' Hartford said again. 'It's me.'

'What do you want?' Joe lowered the shotgun and sat down heavily in the rocker, keeping the shotgun across his knees. The effort of standing had been too much. The old man's chest heaved, every breath a struggle.

'Come home for the wedding, Pa,' Hartford said gently. 'And to see you.'

His father watched him. If he wanted to say anything, the tightness in his chest made it impossible. He rested his head against the back of the chair, half closed his eyes and concentrated on steadying his breathing.

Hartford dismounted and tethered his appaloosa beside the stallion. This close, he could see that the house wasn't in the good state of repair he had first thought. Boards in the porch had rotted and needed replacing; there was termite dust around the foot of the steps and the hitching rail was loose. Inside, the argument was heating up. Hartford could hear some of the words now.

'I told you and told you,' bellowed the older man. 'I forbid it.'

'Sir, please.' The younger man tried to placate him. It was Boone's voice.

Then there was a woman's voice, high and shrill. She protested about something and kept repeating her age. At the same time there was a crash of furniture, more stamping up and down. At first Hartford thought a chair had been upended.

'What's going on?' Hartford drew up a chair beside his pa.

'You got a nerve coming back here.' Pa Hartford's chest buckled as if he was being punched.

'Pa . . .' Hartford couldn't bring himself to contradict the old man. He noticed the black shadows under his eyes, his hollow cheeks and the way his mouth sank slightly at one side.

Inside the house, the argument raged. The woman was in tears now, long wailing sobs of misery. The older man's voice roared like thunder. The younger man, Boone, had given up pleading and shouted back.

'I should shoot you for what you've done.' Joe Hartford's breath tore at his lungs. 'That's what anyone else would do. That's what I would do if we wasn't kin.'

'This about the war?' Hartford kept his question gentle and even. He lowered his eyes and stared at the boards in the porch floor. There was a place where the termites had already made a start.

'Men from round here died because of what you

did.' Joe gripped the arm of the chair until his knuckles were white.

'You don't know what I did.' There was no rise and fall in Hartford's voice, nothing to cause agreement or disagreement.

'Everyone knows what the Pinkertons did. Sided with the Yankees right off. Spied on us. Men died because of it.'

'War's over, Pa.' Hartford refused to catch his eye. 'There's lots of families like ours. People on different sides. They've put their differences aside now.'

'Don't you preach to me.' Joe's hand scrabbled for the shotgun on his lap but the effort of fighting for breath meant he didn't have the strength to grasp it. 'You should have stayed on the farm with me and your brother. Not run off like you did.'

'Nobody ran off, Pa.' Hartford looked him in the eye. 'You know that.'

'The Yankees locked me in jail.' Joe glared at him. His chest heaved. His words snagged in his throat like fishhooks. 'Time I got back here, your Ma was gone.'

Hartford stared at the floor again. He wondered how long the porch floor had left before the termites got all the way through.

'You got termites, Pa,' Hartford said. 'Got to do something.'

'There ain't no termites.' Joe rounded on him, his face and neck mottled red and white as if he was being strangled. 'Place is as sound as a bell.'

The old man's chest lurched. His anger exhausted

him. His grip on the chair relaxed and his arm fell on to his lap, knocking the shotgun on to the porch floor with a clatter. At once, the door burst open and a young woman stood there. The noise of the gun falling had alarmed her. Sounds of the argument between the two men continued inside.

'Johnny?' The woman's face lit up.

Annie had the same chiselled cheekbones as Hartford and if life had given her more of a chance, would have been considered beautiful. But her intelligent blue eyes and fine features were set against ragged hair, roughly tied back, and a cheap, quickly sewn cotton house dress, made as if it was not worth spending time on. Her sleeves were rolled up to the elbows and she looked fatigued and older than her years.

She bobbed down and picked up her father's shotgun and propped it carefully against the wall beside a second gun, which Hartford took to be Boone's. Without thinking, she smoothed her pa's hair and straightened the collar of his shirt. He waved her away crossly, but she didn't seem to notice.

'What are you doing back here?' There were sparks of pleasure in her eyes.

'The wedding,' Hartford said.

'Ah.' Annie bent down and kissed her brother lightly on the cheek.

Hartford took her hand and stared up at her. Inside, the argument seemed to be rumbling to a close. There was an impasse. The curt statements from each of the men, no less angry sounding, were quieter now. The woman's crying had become a continuous sob.

Annie smiled down at Hartford, pleased to let him hold on to her hand.

'What's going on?' Hartford nodded towards the door.

'Oh, just some nonsense.' She smiled again. 'Me and Pa are just fine, ain't we, Pa?' She pulled away from Hartford and let her hand trail lovingly over her father's shoulders, oblivious to the fact that it irritated him.

There was movement inside the house, the sound of furniture being pushed back. The woman stopped crying.

'Pa's getting better,' Annie announced and gave her father's shoulder a gentle squeeze. 'Pleased to see Johnny, ain't you, Pa?'

The old man glared stubbornly ahead as if he hadn't heard. There were blotches of red and white in his face and his breath came in gasps.

Annie was doing what she had always done, Hartford thought, making the best of everything, even when there wasn't anything to make the best of. From as far back as he could remember, she had always been the mortar in the family wall. When Boone was at his angriest, she was the one who persuaded him to talk to Pa. When Ma was worn out with chores, Annie would take over. When Hartford left for Chicago, she made him promise he would write home to Ma. Now she was trying to persuade Pa he was well when he wasn't. The odds being against her had never stopped Annie from trying to do what she thought was for the best. Hartford looked at her tired face and threadbare house dress. He should have thought to bring a present for her and felt a pang of guilt that he had not.

Shouting erupted from inside the house again; the woman screamed. The door was flung open and Boone burst out on to the porch towing a woman behind him.

'Come back here right now.' The older man's anger exploded after them. 'I'm ordering you.'

Boone had the same features as Hartford and Annie, but his eyes were hard and there was an arrogant turn to his mouth. He looked handsome in a new work shirt and hat. He had a silver buckle in the shape of longhorns on his belt and his boots were polished. A new looking Colt .45 was on his hip. He looked delighted with himself, like a kid who had just got away with something. The minute he set foot on the porch, he whooped as if he had just won a prize at a rodeo and the prize was the girl he dragged after him.

A shadow darkened his face the minute he set eyes on Hartford.

'What the hell are you doing back here?'

There was another shout from inside. Boone laughed and without waiting for Hartford to answer, snatched up his shotgun, which was propped by the door, and dragged the girl down the porch steps across the yard in the direction of the barn.

'He's come back for your wedding, Boone,' Annie called.

39

The girl yanked her hand free of Boone's grip and seemed to see Hartford for the first time.

'Our wedding?'

'Come on now, Mary May.' Boone made an angry attempt to grab her hand, but she pulled away and stood looking up at the porch.

'This is our brother Johnny,' Annie smiled proudly. 'Come back from Chicago.'

'Chicago?' Mary May sounded impressed.

Mary May was fresh-faced and pretty, with a touch of rouge on her cheeks and a fine cotton blouse with delicate lacework down the front tucked into her long black skirt.

She seemed genuinely curious to meet someone new because, at twenty-one years old, it seemed to her that she had lived the same dull ranch life forever. She was bored with constant reprimands because she had failed to live up to her father's expectations. Novelty attracted her because it meant excitement.

'Come on, Mary May.' Boone was insistent.

She let him grab her hand this time and pull her in the direction of the barn.

'Where are you headed?' Disappointed, Annie called after them.

A man emerged from the doorway of the house. He wore an expensive black jacket with ribbon edging on the lapels, a thin bow tie and black britches. There was a gold signet ring on a finger of his left hand. He was heavily built and the greying side whiskers which joined in a loop under his nose

40

made it look as if his face was fixed in a permanent scowl. His cheeks were burning. As he glared after Boone and his daughter, his anger was palpable. No one ever got the better of him.

'Damnit,' Dunmore cursed under his breath. 'Just don't know what's got into her.'

'I could make you some coffee, Mr Dunmore,' Annie offered, always the peacemaker.

At that moment, Boone burst out of the stable at the gallop. Mary May was mounted up behind him, clinging to his waist with one hand while the other held the shotgun. As they passed the porch and headed out of the yard, Boone gave a cowboy yell and Mary May laughed with the thrill of it all, her hair flying in the wind.

As the sound of their hoof beats faded, Dunmore's hands clenched into fists. A granite scowl was carved on his face.

'That good-for-nothing boy of yours. . . .' Dunmore rounded on Joe Hartford.

Joe was leaning back in his chair, his mouth open, breath catching in his throat.

'He deserves the hiding of his life. Looks like I'm going to be the one to give it to him.'

'Mr Dunmore . . .' Annie made another attempt.

Dunmore ignored her, clattered down the porch steps and heaved himself up in to the saddle of his black mare.

'Mr Dunmore.' Hartford stood up. 'I'd like a word.'

'I've got enough problems without all this.'

Dunmore refused to listen. 'The ranch is a hornet's nest. Had to fire three of the hands and now the rest of them are demanding a raise. Someone's cutting the herd, I'm losing money and now my daughter is making a fool of herself.'

'Mr Dunmore, wait,' Hartford tried again.

'Do you think I've got time to stay talking here?' Dunmore wheeled his horse. 'Ranch doesn't run itself. If my daughter comes back here, tell her to head home right away.'

'Mr Dunmore,' Annie called after him. 'They're getting married at the weekend. Please stay and talk.'

Dunmore jabbed his heels into the sides of the mare and it leapt forward. He did not look back.

During the early afternoon, while their pa dozed in his chair, Hartford and Annie exchanged news. Annie was thrilled not only to have her brother back home but to have his undivided attention. True to her optimistic nature, she painted a rosy picture of life on the farm. It was a good thing that they no longer had cattle and sheep because she wouldn't be able to cope with them, she said, but she could manage the chickens, the goat and the vegetable garden just fine.

Annie also insisted that it was a good thing that Boone had taken a job in Dallas. While it meant that he was away from home for weeks on end, his wage allowed him to contribute to the household some-times. She aimed to go to Dallas herself one day, she said. Her face lit up as she retold Boone's stories about all the grand houses that were being built there, some of them three storeys high. They were even planning to build an iron bridge over the Trinity River and maybe Boone would get a job working on it.

With Boone away, Annie had become friends with Mary May. She came over almost every day. It was obvious that Mary May didn't get on too well with her pa, but Annie was sure it wasn't anything that couldn't be fixed. The wedding was a different matter, though. Dunmore had outright forbidden it, so Mary May and Boone had gone ahead and made plans anyway. They had a travelling preacher coming and Boone was going to throw a party at the saloon in town because they couldn't hold a reception out at the Lazy D.

'Boone's still got his wild side. But it's only his way, his sense of humour.' Annie smiled to herself, deaf to the excuses she was making. 'You know what he's like. It's always fun first with Boone.'

It was a relief for Annie to have Hartford to talk to. Over plates of bean soup and sourdough, stories flooded out of her – everything from gossip she had picked up at the store, how expensive things had gotten recently, the tricks she used to keep body and soul together when Boone forgot to contribute to the household finances and what Mary May had told her about life at the Lazy D. She spoke in a whisper about Pa's good days and bad days, how the only thing that seemed to give him any sort of pleasure was being taken out in the old buggy and how the lung disease he picked up during his incarceration in the prison camp had worsened year on year since the war ended.

Annie pressed her brother for details of what Chicago was like and his adventures working for the Pinkertons. In return, he thrilled her with descriptions of fine town houses, wide streets, shops, streetcars and city fashions. Then he told stories of gangs of robbers, horseback chases and shoot-outs in railway yards. Wide-eyed, Annie drank in every word.

Pa Hartford slept for two hours straight and woke up angry. He stonewalled Annie's insistence that he should eat and demanded she took him out for a ride. The old man barely glanced at Hartford, let alone spoke to him. His breathing was torture; it seemed like his ribs were going to crack under the strain. Annie's helpless look made it clear that Hartford's presence wasn't helping. He left his sister trying to persuade Joe that he had to eat, assured her he would see her soon, climbed on to his appaloosa and headed back to town.

The afternoon was past its best by the time Hartford left his horse at Greely's livery and strolled back down to the saloon. The heat had begun to lift and a warm wind from the south bowled tumble-weeds through the dirt and made the air smell of prairie sage. Sheriff Milton hurried out of his office and called out to Hartford.

'Pearl said you were out at the farm.' He dispensed with any kind of greeting. 'Mary May Dunmore out there?'

44

'She was . . .' Hartford started to explain.

'I got bad news,' the sheriff said. 'Her pa's been shot dead up at Snake's Creek.'

FOUR

'Poor girl.' Sheriff Milton leaned against the side of his horse and held on to the horn of his saddle. 'Delivering bad news is the worst of this job.'

He was a heavily built man, strong for his years. A steel watch chain was looped across his vest and the tin star pinned to his shirt was dull and edged with rust. His heavy grey moustache was yellowed with nicotine. Under the shadow of his hat, his sharp eyes missed nothing. The lines on his face showed he was used to smiling, but right now his face was stone.

'Been at the farm all morning?'

'Rode out from town about ten,' Hartford said.

'Notice anything untoward?'

'Untoward?' Hartford knew the sheriff was sizing him up, Joe's boy who had gone off to Chicago.

'That fellow I threw in jail, he's gone,' Sheriff Milton said. 'Couple of friends of his waltzed into my office, helped themselves to the keys and busted him out.'

Hartford sensed steely determination in the

46

sheriff. He would never show it, but this was a personal slight. The fellow *I* threw in jail, busted into *my* office. He remembered Milton from when he had been growing up. The whole town relied on him. He faced down rowdy trail hands in the saloon, confiscated their side arms and locked them up for the night. He even had the knack of persuading them it was for their own good so they went without a fuss. Equally, the townsfolk knew that if they had a grievance, a word in Sheriff Milton's ear would get it sorted. His office became a kind of local courtroom where the sheriff's word was law and both parties would leave understanding the reasonableness of whatever decision he arrived at.

'I'll help you look for him,' Hartford said. 'Any idea where he's headed?'

'You sure you didn't notice anything?' Milton wasn't prepared to let anyone off the hook at this stage. 'What about your pa? He'll have been sitting on that porch all morning. See anyone come by? Annie notice anyone?'

Hartford told the sheriff what had happened at the farm, about the argument, how angry Dunmore was, Boone and Mary May riding off.

'Heard Boone took a job in Dallas,' Sheriff Milton said casually. 'Hard work but good money.'

'No one's taken care of the farm for years, looks like,' Hartford said. 'Annie says he helps out with money when he can.'

'Reckon that's where he's headed now?' The sheriff dangled the question like bait. Hartford could see him thinking Boone's your brother, you sure you don't know?

'Raising a posse?' Hartford wanted to show he was on the sheriff's side.

'Take too long.' The sheriff dismissed the suggestion. 'You and me best head straight out to the Lazy D. Mary May might have gone there.'

The Lazy D bordered Joe Hartford's farm. When Joe, Henry Milton, their wives and a handful of other settlers arrived to stake their claims and build a town, they found Dunmore already there. Having arrived a few years before, being ambitious enough for ten men and because there was no competition at that time, he had persuaded the Government Land Agents to part with a generous allocation, miles of prime longhorn country. When they were reluctant to part with a particular land package, he annexed it anyway.

There was no crossbreeding with Herefords back then, the Goodnight-Loving and the Chisholm trails were not yet open, the rail road had not reached Abilene and the farmers across the state line had not taken against them. It was all longhorns, rough riding and the Shawnee trail to Missouri.

After a few short years accumulating his spread, Dunmore's credit was extended to breaking point. The banks which had been pleased to offer mortgages to this hard driving young cattleman now lost their nerve. They began to realize that Dunmore was playing off one mortgage lender against another, robbing Peter to pay Paul. They called in some of his unsecured loans and, when he ignored them, threat-ened foreclosure. Dunmore was livid. He could see his dream of reigning over a cattle empire disappear before his eyes.

Then a young man named Joe Hartford who had recently arrived in the area made him an offer for a patch of land. At first Dunmore was suspicious. It had taken a lot of effort by fair means and foul in order to get his hands on his spread and he didn't want anyone worming their way in. But Joe Hartford seemed a dogged kind of guy, the right sort of per-sonality for a sodbuster, Dunmore thought. His offer showed he wasn't prepared to go above the overdraft his bank had set, which proved to Dunmore that Joe Hartford's ambition was limited to establishing a small farm. He would never be a threat to the Lazy D. So Dunmore sold him the acres he wanted, a patch of land in the north of his property a few miles from Credence. By this time, the Lazy D extended for so many square miles that it didn't matter to Dunmore which part of the property Hartford made an offer on.

True to his cautious nature, Joe Hartford had spent many days out on the Lazy D looking for just the right place to site his farm. On the face of it, the property was open prairie except for the strip of fertile land that bordered the Blue River, which carried enough water for the whole spread even in dry years. He knew there was no point in making Dunmore an offer for any land which bordered the river, so he looked elsewhere.

Under pressure from the banks, Dunmore was wholly concerned with negotiating extensions to his loans and trying to turn his longhorns into profit. He got to the point where he just wanted Joe Hartford to pick out a patch of land, make him a decent offer which would allow him to fend off the banks for the rest of the season and have done with it.

Eventually, Joe Hartford settled on a hundred and fifty acres on the northern boundary of the Lazy D. With the banks on his back, Dunmore was so relieved to close the deal, he didn't bother to enquire why Joe had settled on this particular acreage rather than any other part of his spread. Privately, he believed that no part of the Lazy D was suitable for farming apart from the area close to the Blue River and that Joe's farm would fail within a year or two. In fact, he was so confident of this he insisted on a buy-back clause in the sale agreement and believed Joe was even more gullible than he had first thought when he did not object.

Joe Hartford studied the landscape around the northern part of the property. He noticed the dry river bed, gullies, layers of sedimentary rock and patterns of erosion. He took particular account of the groups of bald cypresses and rusty blackhaws and where patches of dried-up sage gave way to swathes of turkey foot and buffalo grass. He was convinced this was a good place to sink wells and believed he might even find an underground stream. He kept quiet about this during his discussions with Dunmore and was non-committal about his reasons for settling on this particular spot. It

was only months later, when Joe Hartford had success-
fully sunk wells, started to dig irrigation ditches and
sure enough uncovered a stream that Dunmore saw
that he had underestimated his new neighbour. No
matter. The sale had pacified the banks, got the Lazy
D out of a jam and allowed Dunmore to concentrate
on building his empire.

Once they were out of town, Milton rode up alongside Hartford.

'Still with the Agency?'

'They should have let you know I was coming.'
Hartford pulled open his jacket and showed him the
Pinkerton badge. 'Chicago office received a request
for help from Mr Dunmore at the Lazy D Ranch. I'm
supposed to make contact with you and meet
Dunmore on Monday. Came down a couple of days
early for the wedding.'

'Let me guess.' The sheriff's eyes narrowed. 'He's
complaining that someone has been cutting his
herd. The way things usually go, a rider will arrive
from Fort Worth tomorrow to tell me you'll be arriving today.'

Hartford smiled.

'Do well to keep that thing hidden.' The sheriff
indicated his badge. 'Lot of guys round here were in
the 8th Cavalry under General Johnston. Saw action
at Woodsonville, Shiloh, Chattanooga, all over. Most
of them never came back.'

'War's not over then?' Talk of the war irritated
Hartford. It had been at the back of every conversation he had since he arrived.

'It's over,' Sheriff Milton said firmly. 'Folks just don't like to be reminded, that's all.'

'What about you, Sheriff?' Hartford wasn't prepared to let it lie. If he was to work with Milton, he didn't want any barriers between them.

'Joined Hood's brigade with your pa. Took a bullet at Antietam.' The sheriff answered the question matter-of-factly, no resentment in his voice. 'Did you know Dunmore made your pa an offer for the farm?' The sheriff changed the subject. Hartford noticed he hadn't asked about his own war service.

'Recently?' Hartford tried to figure out what this meant. Why hadn't his pa mentioned it?

'If he didn't tell you about it, I guess that means he turned it down.'

The land was dead flat here. Wind lifted a veil of dust out of the sage and toyed with it, covering the clothes, hands and faces of the two men, dried their lips and stung their eyes. The late afternoon sun hammered down on their shoulders. They pulled their hats down low and squinted into the distance where the heat tricked their vision, the air barrelled and spiralled and nothing seemed like it was.

What kind of offer had Dunmore made his pa? The question gnawed at Hartford. Dunmore was the kind of guy who didn't stop until he got what he wanted. What the hell was he doing, leaning on a sick man to sell his life's work? Did this have something to do with the wedding? Was it some kind of ploy to kick Joe Hartford off his land so his Boone wouldn't have a home to come to and his headstrong daughter's wedding plans would fade away?

'Farm's falling apart. Your pa can't work no more. Good land is going to waste.' The sheriff seemed to read Hartford's mind. 'You're gone. Boone's gone now. That only leaves Annie.'

'This offer anything to do with the wedding?' Hartford came out with it.

'Boone and Mary May?' The sheriff concentrated on a spot on the horizon.

'They first ran in to each other as soon as Boone came back from the army. 'Course, there was no one back here then. Your pa was away, Dunmore was away. Your ma was sick with Annie looking after her. Mary May was living out at the Lazy D on her own with the maid. There was Pearl at the saloon holding the town together. If it hadn't been for her, I reckon the whole place would have starved to death.

'She's the one who turned the saloon into a convalescent home for the wounded and made sure everyone had enough to eat. Salt of the earth, that girl. If I had call for a deputy, I'd have her.' The Sheriff's face darkened as he went on with his story. 'Boone got hit in the shoulder at Gaines. Wasn't more than a flesh wound, I saw it myself. Anyhow, he took it on himself to head for home to recuperate.'

'Deserted?' Hartford heard something behind the sheriff's words.

'Let's just say that wound must have taken a long time to heal because he never rejoined the line.' The sheriff's meaning was clear.

'Pearl's pa never came back, did he?' Whenever

Hartford thought about the war, his head filled with the nightmare of all the bloodshed. As Credence was untouched by the fighting, he never considered what it must have been like back here.

'Dunmore managed to get himself back here before the President's Proclamation,' the sheriff went on. 'Herd was scattered. He spent weeks rounding them up. 'Course, who was to say if a few of his neighbours' beeves got mixed in amongst them.' Once again, the sheriff spoke in his roundabout way. 'Heard he turned a fine profit that first season after the war.'

Underfoot, ragged sagebrush gave way to thin buffalo grass. Woken by the vibration of their hoof-beats, yellow-backed scorpions buried themselves under stones and a grey-green prairie rattler uncoiled itself and slid off the trail.

As they drew near to the Lazy D, Hartford noticed the sheriff search the horizon for a sign of approaching riders and turn in his saddle to check the trail behind them. No one there, but he was making sure.

'Who's running things out here now?' Hartford said.

'Foreman's called Charlie Nudd, Jake's brother. Don't expect him to be pleased to see us. Sure will be glad to find Mary May,' the sheriff added. 'Can't stand the thought of her running round somewhere without knowing about her pa.'

Up ahead, they could see a high gateway decorated with pairs of longhorns. Beyond it stood a collection of buildings, a single-storey ranch house

54

with a porch running all the way round it. No cottonwood construction like Joe Hartford's farm house, this was built of expensive pine brought in from the east. Seasoned and treated, the wood glowed like polished leather in the late afternoon sun. Beyond the ranch house were barns, a forge and an acre of cattle pens, all in good repair. There was smoke rising from the forge chimney and the regular clank of a blacksmith's hammer. A couple of men were working on extending the cattle pens, but they were too far away to hear Hartford and the sheriff approach. Hartford looked for Boone's horse at the hitching rail outside the house, but it wasn't there.

'When we find the foreman, let me do the talking.' The sheriff slowed his horse as he approached the gate. 'Charlie Nudd is a good cattleman, but he's got a temper. Worked out here since before the war. He's loyal to Dunmore, joined the regiment with him and came back here afterwards. He won't be regarding me as his best buddy right now.'

A rider was heading towards them from the cattle pens. He approached at an unnecessary gallop and reined his horse in hard. He looked as though he was just back from the herd. His work shirt, hat and pants were covered in dust. He scowled at Hartford and the sheriff as though they had interrupted him in the middle of something and he couldn't wait to get rid of them.

'Come to see Miss Dunmore,' Sheriff Milton announced firmly.

'Rode out this morning, ain't been back all day.' The man sized up Hartford, noticed the Colt on his hip.

'I want to talk to Charlie Nudd then,' Milton said.

'Really, Sheriff?' The man turned his glare back to Milton. 'What makes you think Charlie wants to talk to you?'

FIVE

Hartford and Sheriff Milton stayed outside the gate while the ranch hand walked his horse back to the Lazy D buildings in search of the foreman. Deliberately slow, it seemed to Hartford.

'We should just ride in there,' Hartford snapped.

'No point in riling them from the get-go.' The sheriff sat back in his saddle.

A breeze carried the shouts of the men building the new cattle pens and the monotonous clang of the blacksmith's hammer in the forge. The sun burned their shoulders and the sky was as pale as porcelain. A pair of vultures wheeled patiently overhead.

A man trotted his horse up from the cattle pens. He was short and powerfully built, with muscular shoulders and a chest like a barrel. His work clothes were dirty, and the brim of his old hat was curled where he was in the habit of grabbing it to urge on the beeves when he was out with the herd. He was a grafter. His work was everything to him and now the sour look on his face reminded Hartford and the sheriff that they were calling him away from it.

'Didn't mean to interrupt you, Charlie.' Sheriff Milton was at his most diplomatic.

'What do you want, Sheriff?' He looked at Milton with unqualified loathing.

'Come out to talk to Miss Mary May,' Milton said. 'Got something real important to tell her.'

'Billy told you she ain't here.' Charlie's gaze hardened. 'What did you call me over for?'

'Going to let us in, Charlie?' Milton asked.

'Let you in, hell.' Charlie's grip tightened on his reins. 'You threw Jake in jail for no reason at all.'

'I don't want to argue with you, Charlie,' Milton said softly. 'Dunmore's dead and your brother's busted out of jail. I want you to let us in so we can see for ourselves that Miss Mary May ain't here.'

A guillotine seemed to fall behind Charlie's eyes and cut off his power of speech. He looked panicked and turned from the sheriff to Hartford and back again.

'Where have you been all day, Charlie?' The sheriff's voice was not much more than a whisper but there was steel in it.

Hartford got down off his horse, opened the gate and let the sheriff ride in. Charlie didn't protest.

'Where have you been, Charlie?' Milton repeated.

'Me? Here. Why? What are you saying?' There was some terrible implication in the question but Charlie couldn't figure what it was.

'All day?' The sheriff drew his horse up alongside Charlie's.

'Rode out to gather up a couple of strays. Apart from that I've been here.' Charlie looked winded. 'You say Dunmore's dead?'

'Take us up to the house, Charlie. Got to see Mary May ain't there with my own eyes.'

Charlie wheeled his horse. The sheriff and Hartford rode alongside.

'Where did you find the strays?' Hartford asked.

'Snake's Creek. Why?' Charlie seemed to see Hartford for the first time. 'Who the hell are you anyway?'

'Hartford.'

'Joe Hartford's son?' Charlie puzzled something out. 'The one who ran off and joined the Pinkertons?' He wheeled round and faced the sheriff. 'You brought the Pinkertons in on this?' Charlie put two and two together and made five. 'You think Jake busted out of jail, killed Dunmore and you brought in the Pinkertons?'

'Dunmore was killed up at Snake's Creek,' Hartford said simply.

Charlie stared first at him, then at the sheriff.

'What the hell are you saying?' Charlie went on the attack. He leaned forward and crooked his arms slightly, fists clenched like a boxer closing on his opponent. 'First you accuse Jake, now you're accusing me? You know Dunmore had enemies all over. No one had a good word for him. Ask any of the guys here, they'll tell you.'

'Back up, Charlie. Nobody's accusing anybody,' Milton said quickly. Hartford saw that the sheriff was

59

annoyed that he had rattled Charlie's cage. It wasn't his way. 'And before you get all soured about it, I locked you brother up because Mr Dunmore told me he'd been cutting the herd. He was so hungover he couldn't remember where he was, couldn't even tell me what he'd been celebrating. Those other two clowns both said he was with them, trouble was they were both in different places.'

Charlie slipped easily out of his saddle as they reached the ranch house. The others followed and hitched their horses to the rail. The place was built like a rock. The porch floor was made with two-inch boards, the house walls were twelve-inch diameter pine trunks, neatly sawn with precisely cut joints. The men's boot heels clacked on the solid steps.

'I'll wait here,' Charlie said. 'I don't go in the house in my work clothes.'

The main living room smelled of wood smoke and cigars. A wide, leather-topped desk strewn with papers faced windows which looked south over the full spread of the Lazy D. An oak arm chair stood a couple of feet back from the desk, as if someone had been sitting there and just got up. Over the fireplace hung a pair of prize longhorns, even bigger than the ones that decorated the main gate. There were a pair of balloon-backed chairs beside the hearth, each with an oil lamp on an occasional table. The stained wooden floor as well as the wooden vaulted ceiling made the room dark.

The rest of the ranch house was deserted. Everything was neat, everywhere was swept, polished and clean and the beds were made. In what was obviously Mary May's room, a beautiful new cotton dress lay on the bed ready for her to put on. In the kitchen, the stove was lit as if someone was expecting to cook a meal. Outside the back door in the yard, chickens pecked at the handfuls of grain which had been scattered for them. Hartford and the sheriff found Charlie Nudd perched on the front step, nervously turning his hat in his hands.

'Told you no one was there, didn't I?'

'Who looks after the place?' Hartford said.

'Blacksmith's wife does the cooking and cleaning.' Charlie stared out across the yard.

'What's Mary May like, Charlie?' Sheriff Milton sat down on the step beside him. He made it sound as if he was asking the question in confidence. 'You've been here a long time. You know everybody.'

'What do you mean?' Charlie's face turned puce.

'Just trying to get a picture, that's all.' Milton shrugged. 'You must have practically grown up together.'

'What are you saying? I never grew up with her.' Not being able to see what the sheriff was driving at made Charlie's temper flare.

'I just mean how is she going to take the news about her pa?' The sheriff was patience itself.

'Hell, I don't know.' Charlie caught Hartford's eye. 'Spends her time running round with your brother Boone, that's all I know.'

'What about Boone?' Hartford chipped in.

'Ain't no good for her, that's all I know. I don't

care if he is your brother or no.' Charlie's face was flint. 'They went around boasting to everyone they were getting hitched. When Mr Dunmore found out about it, he was mad as hell.'

'Were you sweet on Mary May, Charlie?' the sheriff asked softly. The question sounded good-humoured, a fond old uncle teasing a favourite nephew.

Charlie leapt to his feet as if he'd been snakebit. His face was on fire. He made sure he didn't look at either Hartford or the sheriff, mumbled something about having to get back to work and that they should close the gate when they left. He launched himself into his saddle and spurred his pony in the direction of the cattle pens without another word.

It was Hartford's instinct to follow Charlie. He wanted to see the lie of the ranch, see who else worked there, discover the reaction of the men when they heard what had happened to their boss. And the sheriff's question about Mary May puzzled Hartford. It was something it would never have crossed his mind to ask. The young foreman had secretly carried a torch for the boss's daughter. So what? He wouldn't be the first. Or the last.

One thing was clear, Hartford reckoned. Annie's letter, which had described how thrilled folks were over the wedding plans, was wishful thinking. The only people who were excited about the event were the couple and Annie herself. Pearl may have strung a few paper streamers around the saloon but Pa Hartford hadn't mentioned it, Dunmore was against it, Charlie Nudd was hostile and Boone obviously wasn't expecting his brother to turn up.

'I'm going after him,' Hartford said. Charlie had reached the cattle pens and had called a group of men away from their work.

'Why?' Milton said. 'Charlie's as angry as a ball of spit right now. He ain't going to tell you anything.'

'What about the other guys? There must be ten at least who work here.'

'What are you going to ask?' the sheriff said. 'What are they going to tell you?'

'Look, Sheriff, I got a job to do, just like you.' The easy manner of the older man had begun to irritate him.

Milton followed Hartford down the porch steps to their horses. He grimaced with pain as he heaved himself up into his saddle and waited for Hartford to go on. Down by the cattle pens, Charlie was talking intently to the guys. As they watched, men who had been working further away downed tools and came running. Charlie turned and pointed in the direction of Hartford and the sheriff. All the men stared at them as if they were the proof of what he had been saying.

'I got to go and talk to them,' Hartford repeated.

'Leave it,' the sheriff edged his horse close to Hartford's. 'They ain't in the mood for talking.'

The sound of hammering stopped abruptly and a giant of a man in a blacksmith's apron emerged from the forge and joined them. A woman hurried along behind him. Charlie launched into a more animated explanation and the blacksmith too stared in the direction of Hartford and the sheriff.

'Come on.' The sheriff turned his horse towards the ranch gate.

Hartford took a hard look at the men. Pinkerton training made him note of how many there were and etch the details of what they looked like into his brain so he would be able to recognize them again.

'See to the gate, will you? I don't want to get down out of this saddle if I don't have to.'

'How come you needled Charlie like that, sheriff?' The sheriff's line of questions had hardly seemed relevant to Hartford. 'We needed to talk to the hands, not just him. Now he's lined them all up against us. Makes our job harder.'

'Dunmore treated Charlie like a favourite son. Took him on when he was fourteen years old. Looked after him in the army, so I heard. Now he's promoted him to foreman.' The sheriff slowed his horse to a walking pace.

Pools of evening shadow appeared at the base of the sage, the saguaro flowers loosened slightly in anticipation of the coming darkness. The trail dirt which had reflected the sunlight like a mirror earlier in the day was dull now and in the east, a blueberry stain soaked the edge of the sky. With momentary curiosity, a family of jack rabbits watched them pass then chased off somewhere amongst the brush. From far off came the yelping of a lone coyote.

'One thing you don't know,' the sheriff continued quietly. 'Dunmore cut Charlie into his will, left him a stake in the place. Told me so himself.'

Hartford tried to figure what this meant.

'Old Dunmore was beaten up by the thought of his darling Mary May running around with your brother. The day after she told him to his face she was going to marry him, he rode up to Dallas and found himself a lawyer. And there it was in black and white.'

'He told you?' Hartford had to be sure.

'Showed me,' Milton said. 'Stopped by my office on his way home. Guys like Dunmore, who are in charge of running things don't generally have anyone to talk to. The whole thing was driving him crazy, so he stopped by and spilled the whole thing. A quarter share in the Lazy D will keep Charlie for the rest of his natural days and some.'

'And Charlie was up at Snake's Creek today,' Hartford said. 'So what was this about Charlie having sweet thoughts for Mary May?'

'Wasn't much of a guess.' Milton laughed to himself. 'She was the only girl up on that ranch.'

'Doesn't mean a thing.' Hartford shook his head. 'Every guy on the Lazy D will have had pictures of Mary May in his head.'

'What if Charlie had asked Dunmore for Mary May's hand. . . .'

'That's bull, Sheriff, and you know it,' Hartford cut across him. He had never heard anything so ridiculous. 'Charlie's a ranch hand. You reckon Dunmore would stand by while he makes a play for his daughter? Never in a thousand years. Anyway, so what if he did?'

'Charlie was like a son to Dunmore. After all, he was going to inherit a quarter share.' The sheriff reined in his horse and stood facing Hartford. 'What if Charlie got greedy? What if he wanted it all? What if he did ask Dunmore if he could marry Mary May? He'd have it all then, Mary May and the whole of the Lazy D. Thing is, how would he react if Dunmore turned him down?'

SIX

The sheriff reached into his desk drawer and brought out a bottle of red eye and two glasses. Hartford pulled up a chair. Outside, the street was filled with the grainy light of early dusk. As the sheriff lit the oil lamp that stood on the desk, an orange glow filled the room, the whiskey shone like brass and the window darkened until the street became invisible and the room was reflected in a sheet of polished jet. A set of heavy iron keys lay on the desk and the cell door was open.

'So Dunmore asked you guys for help.' The sheriff poured the whiskey and pushed a glass over to Hartford. 'Because the local law enforcement wasn't no good.'

'He never said that.' By now, Hartford was used to the oblique way the sheriff asked questions. 'Told us someone had been cutting the herd and no one could get to the bottom of it. He offered to pay the salary of an agent, if Chicago would send one down. Said you'd been looking into it.'

'Well, that's true enough.' The sheriff reflected for a moment. Hartford noticed that he had not yet touched his whiskey.

'Told you I came down a couple of days early when Annie wrote to me about the wedding.'

'Someone's been cutting Dunmore's herd all right.' The sheriff leaned back in his chair. 'Same as every herd between here and Kansas. You're talking about hundreds of square miles of open range, cattle constantly being moved from grazing to grazing, every cowpoke as poor as dirt, every rancher willing to buy beeves on the cheap. This is how it is down here, you know that.' The sheriff grimaced as he stretched his legs out under the desk. 'You, me and a whole army of Pinkertons couldn't put a stop to it.'

Hartford knew it was true. Stories of gangs of rustlers lying in wait for the beeves as they were being moved north to the railheads were nonsense believed by city folks, even the ones who ran the Pinkerton Office in Chicago. Down here, ranchers were always anxious to increase their stock and would pay for anything anyone offered them. Odds on, Dunmore was no different. There were probably as many steers in his herd with other ranches' brands on them as the ones he had lost.

'Dunmore suspect anyone?' Hartford asked.

'Dunmore could think of a reason why every cowboy in Credence was the one cutting the herd. Gave me a list of names a yard long. Like to guess who was on the top of that list?'

The lamp flickered and shadows danced crazily

across the ceiling. The sheriff didn't take his eyes off Hartford.

'Your brother, Boone.' The sheriff's words tolled like a funeral knell.

'Dunmore have any evidence?' The whiskey burned in Hartford's gut.

'Told me when it came to a confrontation, Boone just laughed in his face.'

The lamp flickered again. Black shapes danced.

'Early start in the morning.' The sheriff reached for his whiskey and downed it in one. 'I need to find Mary May and there's plenty more questions to ask. After that, we'll try to get a fix on Jake Nudd and the other two. Someone must know where they're headed.'

Over at the saloon, the oil lamp on the bar was lit. Pops Wardell and Bill Greely were sitting with Pearl in a pool of wax-coloured light. The rest of the place was in darkness. As Hartford pushed open the door, he saw Pearl's hand move towards the twelve gauge on her knees. Pops broke off from the story he had been telling them and the three of them stared towards him.

'Gun,' Pearl called out to him. 'One rule for everybody, Hart.'

Hartford unbuckled his gun belt and hung it on the peg by the door.

'Just telling 'em how I found the body.' Judging by the frozen expressions on the others' faces, Pops must have told the story half a dozen times.

'Damnedest thing,' Pops launched straight into

the story again without asking if anyone wanted to hear it. 'Headed straight up to Snake's Creek this afternoon. There's pools up there where they got flat-head carp fat as your arm. Been going up there for years.'

'You want a drink, Hart? Something to eat?' Pearl interrupted the story. 'I got a cold beef stew out back.'

'Stew would be fine.' Hartford suddenly remembered he hadn't eaten all day.

Pearl slipped down off her bar stool. Pops continued without missing a beat.

' 'Course I never saw him at first. Headed down the bank to my usual spot and there he was. Right there in front of me, lying on his back in the reeds. Eyes wide open staring up at me.' Pops paused to judge the effect of this on his audience.

Greely clearly relished the story even though he had heard it before. His lopsided grin showed black teeth.

'Bet you thought he was alive,' Greely said excitedly. His favourite part was coming next.

'Thought he was staring straight at me,' Pops went on. 'Thought he was alive and was lying there watching me.'

Greely gave a little excited whoop. He'd never heard anything so good.

'Bet you talked to him too.' Greely's eyes nearly popped out of his head. 'What did you say?'

'I said howdy, Mr Dunmore, what are you doing down there?'

'Howdy, Mr Dunmore,' Greely echoed and slapped his skinny thigh with sheer delight, his black grin a mile wide. 'Damndest thing I ever heard, saying howdy to a corpse.'

'I didn't know he was dead.' Not wanting to be shown up in front of Hartford, Pops glared at Greely. 'Not right then.'

'You haven't said about his horse,' Greely prompted him. He caught Hartford's eye, letting him know that as a livery man, horses were his concern.

'What about his horse?' Pops had lost the thread.

'Dunmore's horse,' Greely sounded disappointed that he had to remind his friend. He turned to Hartford to explain. 'Black mare. I've looked after her in the livery.'

'Oh yeah,' Pops remembered. He looked knowingly at Hartford. 'Horse was standing right there. Refused to move.'

'Loyal,' Greely explained. 'More loyal than dogs, horses. Most folks don't know that.'

The interruption made Pops lose where he was again.

'Tracks,' Greely sounded disappointed. He wanted Pops to get back into the swing of the story so he could enjoy it.

'I was coming to that,' Pops said crossly. Greely was stealing his thunder. He turned to Hartford. 'There were fresh tracks all heading towards McGreggor's spread. That's an indication of something, ain't it?'

John McGreggor was Dunmore's neighbour to the

east. His vast ranch occupied hundreds of square miles of cattle country right up to the Trinity River. Whereas Dunmore's domination of this part of Texas was respected, McGreggor ruled his land like an emperor. He had a reputation for dispensing acts of charity, cruelty and summary justice on a whim.

Over the years, McGreggor and Dunmore had rubbed along. With their ranch houses a few hours' ride apart, they didn't have to see each other if they didn't want to and rarely ran into each other by accident. Although each of them had an idea in his head of where the boundary between their two properties lay, they probably would have been hard pressed to draw an accurate line on the ground. No matter. It was wide open country and there was room enough for them both.

When each of these two barons came back from the war and set their men to gathering up their respective herds, each accepted that this would mean incursions into the other's property. Dunmore ended up with steers bearing McGreggor's brand amongst his herd and vice versa. As many of the cattle had bred in the years the men were away and carried no brand at all, neither complained. But when the Shawnee Trail closed, everything changed.

In August 1866, President Johnson's Proclamation declared that '. . . insurrection is at an end and peace, order, tranquillity and civil authority now exist throughout the whole of the United States of America.' It may have looked like that from Washington, but down here the country was crawling with embittered, armed, ex-military men who had lost everything. Far from ushering in an era of tranquillity and civil authority, this turned out to be the era of the gunfighter.

Once they had gathered their herds and realized the scale of the profits they could make, both Dunmore and McGreggor eyed up each other's property and the size of each other's herd and privately regretted the easy-come way they had established their boundary before the war.

Another thing that happened was that Dunmore's men who had joined up with him all returned safely to the Lazy D after the war. Most of McGreggor's men who followed him into the army were killed. Dunmore's men settled back in to the ranch life they were used to. McGreggor was forced to hire new men from the assortment of drifters and ex-soldiers who gravitated to the area because they had nowhere else to go. When it came to rounding up his herd, McGreggor saw that he could turn this to his advantage. His new hands could not have cared less about which steers carried the McGreggor brand and which did not and when it came to snatching longhorns from Dunmore's property, most of them didn't even know where the boundary was.

When they closed the Shawnee, trouble between the cattlemen came to a head. For months, relations between them had been deteriorating. Each accused the other of stealing his beeves. When the ranch hands ran into each other on the range, they traded threats. There had been fistfights at the saloon in

Credence and Sheriff Milton had locked up the offenders overnight. This meant fines had to be paid and since the men had blown their meagre wages in the saloon, Dunmore and McGreggor were summoned. Both of them resented having to bail their men out and each of them blamed the other. But the main bone of contention was that with the Shawnee closed, McGreggor had to drive his cattle across Dunmore's land to pick up the Chisholm Trail to head north.

Pearl packed Pops Wardell and Bill Greely off home for the night.

'No one would want Dunmore out of the way more than McGreggor.' Pearl set Hartford's plate of stew in front of him and explained how things stood between the two ranchers.

'Rumour is that McGreggor made Dunmore an offer for the Lazy D and he turned it down. That would have solved his problem about driving his herd to the Chisholm and having to negotiate with Dunmore every year.' Pearl poured herself a glass of red eye from the bottle on the bar.

'Guess all this means the wedding will be off.' Hartford wanted Pearl to tell him about Mary May.

'If it was ever on.' Pearl took a slug of whiskey. 'Boone was supposed to pay me to decorate the place for him, but I ain't seen a nickel yet. Mary May persuaded Dunmore to come in here to look the place over a few weeks ago. They ended up having a scorching row right in front of Pops and Bill Greely. Dunmore yelled that if she got herself hitched without his say so, he'd never speak to her again.'

'Doesn't make sense.' Hartford shook his head.

'Not much does round here,' Pearl laughed. 'Town is dying on its feet and everyone is at each other's throats.'

'So you reckon Boone was just leading Mary May in some kind of dance?' Hartford said. 'Heard Charlie Nudd carries a torch for her too.'

'Poor Charlie.' Pearl shook her head sadly. 'As far as Dunmore was concerned, no guy was ever going to be good enough to marry his daughter. He liked Charlie though, I heard he even cut him into his Will.'

'Could Dunmore have left him a piece of the Lazy D in exchange for him letting Mary May alone?' Hartford wanted to test the sheriff's theory on her.

'Bought him off?' Pearl hesitated. The possibility had never occurred to her. 'Even if he did, it wouldn't have made much difference. Mary May is of a mind to do exactly what she wants to, with or without her Pa's blessing.'

Shadows massed round the pool of yellow lamp-light where Pearl and Hartford sat. The air had cooled now and it was hard to recall what the heat of the day had felt like. Outside the window, a peach coloured moon hung in a cobalt sky and swathes of glittering stars were scattered across the night.

SEVEN

A hand on his shoulder shook Hartford awake. Amongst the shadows, he could just make out the outline of a bulky figure standing over him. Outside the window, moonlight covered the town like a silver shawl and grey, pre-dawn light softened the edge of the sky. Somewhere a rooster screeched to warn that day was coming. Instinctively, Hartford's hand slipped under his pillow and felt for his Navy Colt.

'Pearl's made coffee.' It was Sheriff Milton's voice. 'If we leave now, we should reach McGreggor's spread by mid-morning.'

Downstairs, the saloon was rich with the smell of fresh coffee. Pearl had lit the oil lamp on the bar and a coffee pot, two tin cups and a sourdough loaf waited for them. The men tore off pieces of bread and dipped them. The coffee was bitter and as thick as oil.

Hartford's head was bursting with questions about his pa, Boone, Mary May, Dunmore, McGreggor, all of them. They all boiled down to a single one, he realized: how could things have got so bad? Since the war, everything had got shaken up and tipped on its head. No one got along any more: Dunmore and Joe Hartford were at each other's throats, Mary May hated her pa, Boone was still flying in the face of everybody. The Nudd brothers had once been stalwarts of the Lazy D and now Charlie was bitter and Jake had been thrown in jail. Then there was McGreggor: the truce between him and Dunmore which had lasted for years had broken down. Boone and Mary May had run off somewhere and now Dunmore was dead.

Hartford watched the sheriff blow on his coffee. In the old days, folks brought their disputes to him, respected his impartiality and stuck by his judgement. Now it was different. McGreggor would hardly give him the time of day, Mary May Dunmore hadn't turned to him for help and two cattle hands had had the brass nerve to bust their friend out of jail.

'Pearl's gone to wake up Bill Greely.' The sheriff concentrated on wiping the inside of his coffee cup with a crust of bread. 'He'll bring the horses down from the livery.'

Hartford knew this was to save the sheriff the effort of walking the length of the street on his aching knees.

As they left town, Hartford pulled his jacket tight. Even with hot coffee inside him, the morning cold drove through his clothes. In the east along the horizon, watery dawn light began to prise open the darkness. The horses picked their way between the beehive cactus and Jerusalem thorns that loomed at them out of the shadows.

'Reckon McGreggor could have had Dunmore killed?' It was the one thing Hartford wanted to know above all else.

'If someone wants to do something, he'll always find a reason.' The sheriff sighed wearily. 'Always find a way to make sure his actions are justified. Then he can hold his head up and live with himself and his neighbours.'

'You mean McGreggor believed he had a reason for killing Dunmore?' Hartford was impatient for an answer. The sheriff's roundabout way was too slow him.

Light was coming up fast now. The eastern sky split open and revealed primrose clouds painted with crimson scars. All around them, stones and cactus plants cast black shadows. The dull thud of their horses' hoofs accompanied the jingle of their bridles. But night cold was still in the air, held each of the men in a tight embrace, slipped inside their shirts and froze their bones.

'Another thing you should know,' the sheriff turned to Hartford. 'Jake Nudd, Logan and Clyde Shorter too, all worked on the McGreggor ranch a while back. McGreggor reckoned they was cutting the herd and selling his beeves to Dunmore so he fired them.'

Hartford knew what was coming next. Sheriff Milton's laconic way of telling a story made him smile.

'So Dunmore took them on. From what he told

me, they've been cutting his herd and selling the beeves back to McGreggor.'

'That why you threw Jake Nudd in jail?' Hartford said. 'Is he going to take the fall for all this?'

'Jake ain't got the brains to cut a herd and negotiate the sale of beeves with anyone. I locked him up for his own good. Thought it might take the heat out of the situation. Dunmore was raging mad.' The sheriff paused. 'Anyhow, chances are Dunmore would have given them their jobs back eventually. Why shouldn't he? He didn't have proof against any of them. Then that fool Logan gets it into his head that Dunmore has stitched him up. He decides to bust Jake out to get back at Dunmore, me and anyone else he can think of.'

'Reckon Logan had been cutting Dunmore's herd?' Hartford knew what the sheriff's answer was going to be.

'Put money on it,' the sheriff laughed. 'No one will ever prove it. It would take days to ride out and inspect all the brands on McGreggor's beeves, weeks even. He'd know you were coming before you could get to them. Then you'd find the herd was scattered or suddenly there were strays all over and no one knew where they were. At the very least he'd have had time to change the brands.'

The same morning Dunmore's plea for help had come through to Washington Street, Allan Pinkerton gave the order that an agent should be dispatched. Dunmore complained that rustlers were stealing his livelihood from under him and he had no one to help him. Hartford knew the lie of the land so he was sent.

A case that had seemed as transparent as spring water in the Pinkerton office, down here was like staring into a muddy pool. Everyone wanted something someone else had. Dunmore wanted the Hartford farm. McGreggor wanted Dunmore's spread. Mary May wanted Boone to help her escape from her pa. Charlie Nudd wanted Mary May. The ranch hands were stealing cattle. The list went on.

The boundary between the Lazy D and McGreggor's property came into view sooner than Hartford and the sheriff expected. From a mile away, they could see the posts of a new wire fence stretching out into the distance. A freshly painted sign hung over the gates bearing the legend 'McGreggor' in black capitals. Three horses were tethered to the fence and their riders leaned against the gate. Two of them were smoking cigarettes and the third held a Winchester loosely under his arm.

It was mid morning. The heat was building as usual, in a few hours the place would be a furnace. Wakened by the vibration of the horses' hoofs, a nest of confused and angry scorpions careered about in the dirt, darting this way and that, their stings arched above them ready to strike. The sand-coloured young were almost transparent in the sunlight while the hard-backed adults, no less quick in their movements, tumbled over each other, slaves to their abiding instinct to search out a victim and strike.

'McGreggor move his boundary?' Hartford indicated the new fence.

The men at the gate noticed them. One raised his arm and pointed, a second climbed up the gate rungs to get a better view.

As they drew closer, the sheriff raised his arm and gave a broad wave, a friendly salute. One of the men untied his horse and set off at a gallop back towards the ranch house.

Some time before Hartford and the sheriff reached the two remaining men, they recognized them. Logan held the Winchester and Clyde Shorter stood a couple of feet behind him. The sheriff raised his hand and waved again. Logan shifted the position of the Winchester and held it ready to swing up to his shoulder.

'Far enough, Sheriff,' Logan called out when they were well within range.

Sheriff Milton ignored him and carried on riding until he was up close. Hartford followed. Logan cradled the Winchester under his arm, the barrel levelled at the sheriff's chest.

'Was hoping I'd run into you, Logan.' Sheriff Milton sounded as if he had just dropped by to pass the time.

The more friendly the sheriff sounded, the more the blood beat in Logan's face. He glowered at them. His clothes were immaculate as usual, collar and cuffs perfectly turned, pants pressed and his hat brushed free of dust. His index finger was poised on the trigger guard of the Winchester.

Clyde Shorter looked panicked. His eyes darted from the sheriff to Hartford and back again. He wore a battered old straw hat and rivulets of sweat ran down the side of his face. Damp patches discoloured his baggy cotton shirt. His hand rested on the .45 which was tucked under his stomach in the belt of his pants.

'What do you want, Sheriff?' Logan snapped.

Although Logan was angry, Hartford could see that their presence threw him off balance. Not knowing what to do, he had sent the third man back to the ranch for instructions.

'Was that Charlie Nudd's brother you just sent back to the house?' the sheriff carried on innocently. ''Cause if it was, I heard you did me a favour.'

Logan's stare switched to Hartford as if he could explain what the sheriff was going on about.

'A favour?' Logan echoed. The Winchester wavered in the crook of his arm.

'You help him, Clyde?' The sheriff turned his attention to Clyde Shorter.

'Me?' Shorter's voice came out as a squeak. 'What's he saying, Logan?'

'I said what do you want?' Logan mustered his anger again in an attempt to shift the sheriff's disarming smile.

'Let me ask you fellas something.' Still smiling, the sheriff leaned forward in his saddle and lowered his voice as if he was letting them into a secret. 'Was that Jake Nudd who was standing here with you just now?'

'So what if it was?' Logan growled.

'Then you did me a service.' The sheriff's friendly manner was unshakable. 'Unlocked my jail cell and left the keys on the desk.'

Logan raised the Winchester. He couldn't make sense of anything.

In the far distance beyond the gate, Hartford noticed the dust kicked up by a rider at the gallop. Clyde Shorter turned round to look. Even though the drum of hoof beats was clearly audible, the sheriff didn't take his eyes off Logan.

'Saved me doing the exact same thing. I was heading back to my office to let old Jake out after he'd cooled off after a night on the red eye and what do you know?' The sheriff's eyes twinkled with amusement. 'He was gone.'

'Logan,' Clyde Shorter pulled at Logan's sleeve. The rider would be with them any minute. Shorter looked terrified.

'Asked around in the saloon. They said you and Clyde had high-tailed it, so I put two and two together.'

The rider reached them and reined in his horse, kicking up a cloud of dust.

'Well lookee,' the sheriff crowed. 'Here he is. How are you doing, Jake?'

Jake Nudd looked just as nonplussed as Logan had.

'None the worse for cooling off in my jail?'

'Boss says bring 'em up to the house,' Nudd said to Logan.

Logan nodded sharply to Clyde Shorter to indicate that he should open the gate.

On the way up to the ranch house, the sheriff kept up a stream of friendly banter. He enquired how the guys had been keeping, said how pleased he was to have run into them and emphasised how good it was to see that Jake had suffered no ill effects from his night in the cell. The men replied in gruff monosyllables. As none of them were used to friendly treatment or anyone showing concern for them, they were taken in by the sheriff's repartee. But every time he touched on how grateful he was for them freeing Jake from the jail cell, they exchanged nervous glances.

A quarter mile inside the gate, the ground lifted. When they reached the top of the rise they had their first view of the ranch house and its outbuildings. The house itself was an old Mexican army fort that dated back to the Mexican War. It was a single-storey adobe construction, built round what had once been a parade ground. The lime-washed walls shone in the late morning sun. There were lookout towers at each of the four corners, ramparts running round the tops of the walls and the parade ground was now an emerald green lawn.

Further on, beyond the house stood the usual collection of ranch buildings, workshops, a forge, stables, barn and a wooden bunkhouse for the men. In the distance were cattle pens and way beyond them, a couple of miles out towards the horizon, a cloud of dust hung in the air showing the movement of the herd.

Logan and the others escorted Hartford and the

sheriff under the adobe arch. Once inside, the walls provided shade and the scent of the newly watered grass hung in the air. There were flowers too. A mantle of crimson bougainvillea draped over one wall, a triangular bed of yellow, pink and white roses had been made in a corner of the lawn while in the exact centre stood a lemon tree. The simple beauty of the place was breathtaking.

Logan led the way up one side of the lawn to where an orange-tiled roof shaded a flagstone porch. In awe of the place, none of the men spoke. As they approached the porch, they became aware of two figures, a man and a woman, standing back in the shadows.

'Leave your horses here.' Logan nodded towards a hitching rail.

While Hartford and the sheriff dismounted, Logan and the other men disappeared back towards the main gate. The sheriff turned away from the porch to hide the pain in his face as he eased himself down from his stirrup.

The two figures stepped forward to greet them. Judging by his expensive clothes, Hartford guessed the man was McGreggor. The woman was Mary May.

EIGHT

McGreggor was tall, powerfully built with steel-grey hair combed straight back and a heavy grey moustache. He wore a black jacket, pressed white shirt open at the neck, black pants and black boots with pointed steel toecaps. From where he stood on the porch, he looked down on Hartford and the sheriff as they dismounted. The stern expression on his face showed they were unwelcome.

Mary May was the picture of misery. Hartford remembered her laughter as Boone snatched her away from her father the previous afternoon, a mixture of the delight of a bride-to-be and the over-excitement of a child who has misbehaved. Now her face was tearstained and her hair was a mess. She looked frail and stooped; the effort of holding herself upright took all her strength. She kept close to McGreggor, as if his commanding presence provided her with shelter.

'Mr McGreggor, Miss.' Sheriff Milton touched the

brim of his hat.

McGreggor said nothing. Sullen anger sat in his face as though the arrival of the two men was impertinence.

'Glad to have found you, Miss Dunmore,' the sheriff went on. 'We looked for you out at the Lazy D yesterday.'

'I was at the store.' Mary May looked dazed – merely recalling where she had been the previous afternoon was a struggle. 'Everyone was talking about . . .'

McGreggor took her arm to steady her while she summoned the strength to continue. 'They said some old guy from the saloon had been out at Snake's Creek. He'd seen. . . .' She caught the sheriff's eye and then Hartford's, desperate for them to tell her it wasn't true. 'I headed out to Annie's to get her to ride out there with me, but her pa was so sick, she couldn't leave him.' Mary May hesitated and looked up at McGreggor who still held her arm. 'I didn't know where else to turn.'

'I think you should go inside and rest, my dear.' McGreggor's kindly advice sounded like a command. 'I shall see what Sheriff Milton wants.'

As Mary May obediently withdrew, McGreggor turned coldly to the sheriff. What he really wanted to do was to order him off his property but, with Mary May within earshot, he maintained steely politeness.

'Miss Dunmore is lucky to have you to turn to.' The sheriff's compliment fell on deaf ears. Milton's easygoing manner may have distracted the men at the gate, but McGreggor was more difficult. He looked thunderous.

'Noticed you've been putting up fences,' the sheriff continued as if it was the most natural thing in the world. 'Good strong posts. Those boys who let us in, did they do that?'

'Fences?' McGreggor didn't follow.

'Did a good job.' The sheriff smiled at him. 'Couldn't help noticing, that's all.'

'What are you talking about?' McGreggor prided himself on not suffering fools. He must have misjudged Sheriff Milton – the man was babbling like an idiot.

'Those boys who used to work for Dunmore,' the Sheriff continued cheerfully. 'He had some notion that they'd been cutting his herd. Now they're working for you.'

'What are you saying?' McGreggor was beginning to see where this could lead.

'Had Jake Nudd locked in a cell. The other two let him out without my say-so. Must have headed straight out here.' The sheriff sounded innocently surprised as if the idea had just occurred to him.

'What exactly do you want?' McGreggor looked pained.

'You tell those guys to move the boundary into the Dunmore property?' The sheriff lowered his voice so McGreggor had to strain to hear him. 'Those guys, who cut Dunmore's herd, they offer to sell Dunmore's beeves to you?'

'What?' The sheriff had bundled his questions together so McGreggor couldn't disentangle one from another. He glanced over the sheriff's shoulder to where Logan and the other had passed under the arch.

'Those guys.' The sheriff seemed to weigh his words. 'You can't trust any of them.' He caught McGreggor's eye, letting him in on something for his own good. 'Cutting herds, putting up fences in the wrong place, busting out of jail, I mean . . .' The sheriff's words tumbled out. 'And what about Mary May. Her pa's dead. She's here. Where's the guy she's supposed to be marrying tomorrow?'

Just as McGreggor opened his mouth to answer, the sheriff turned to Hartford.

'We should ask her that? I mean, he's your brother after all.'

Hartford went to say something, but the sheriff wasn't interested. His eye was on McGreggor. The ranch boss was struggling for words on his own luxurious porch. He had the feeling that whatever answer he gave, he was going to incriminate himself and he couldn't figure out why.

'You got anything to say about Dunmore getting shot?' The sheriff let his question hang in the air.

Mary May appeared at McGreggor's side like a shadow. Overhearing the mention of her father's name had brought her out on to the porch again.

'Do you know who did it, Sheriff?' Mary May's eyes were red. Her arms hung helplessly at her sides and one hand held her handkerchief twisted

89

as tight as rope.

'Miss Dunmore, pleased you could come out.' The sheriff touched his hat again. 'I just wanted to clear up one thing. That scattergun you had with you when you left the Hartford farm yesterday, what happened to that? And the answer to your question is no, I'm sorry, not yet we don't.'

'Scattergun?' Not expecting the question, Mary May was lost.

The sheriff shrugged as if it was nothing.

'I don't own a scattergun, Sheriff.' She looked at McGreggor for reassurance.

'Where's Boone?' Hartford said.

Mary May started to cry. She lowered her head and low sobs shook her. McGreggor put a great arm round her narrow shoulders and turned her towards the house.

'Go back inside, my dear. These men are just leaving.'

McGreggor stepped down off the porch and stood face to face with the sheriff.

'Get out now.' His voice rasped in his throat.

'Boone is this man's brother.' The sheriff took a step towards McGreggor. 'He deserves to know where he is.'

'You're the Pinkerton?' McGreggor rested his hand on the door jamb and stared at Hartford. 'You really think that wastrel brother of yours stands a chance with Miss Dunmore?' McGreggor lowered his voice to a whisper. 'She's under my protection now.'

As he headed inside, the steel rims on the heels of his boots sparked against the flagstone floor.

The sheriff struggled to pull himself up on to his horse. As he took his weight on his foot in the stirrup, pain tightened his face.

'You're leaving, just because McGreggor says so?' Hartford was amazed; where there was danger he was used to heading straight into it.

'Man like McGreggor likes to make his own decisions.' The sheriff turned his horse. The lawn was so green against the dusty path, it seemed to shine. 'We've poked him with a stick. Give him a few hours and he'll figure it's his own idea to tell us what he knows.'

Hartford said nothing. He didn't share the older man's faith in the plan and he didn't give a damn about letting McGreggor save face. The sheriff had goaded McGreggor about pushing his boundary into Dunmore's land, but what use was that? What was Mary May doing there? What about Boone? He had it on the tip of his tongue to ask the sheriff if he at least intended to take Jake Nudd back to jail.

As they passed under the adobe arch, Hartford looked back. The whitewashed walls of the house reflected the sunlight, the lawn was vivid green, the place was tranquil. The porch was in shadow and he couldn't see if McGreggor had stepped outside again to watch them leave.

'Tell them at the gate that I went inside with McGreggor,' Hartford said quickly.

Before the sheriff could reply, he had turned his

horse and headed away from the gate and towards the cattle pens. He had to see for himself if Dunmore's steers were down there. After all, these were his orders from Allan Pinkerton. He clicked his tongue to hurry his appaloosa and ignored whatever protest the sheriff called out after him.

It was a quarter mile of dirt track between the house and the pens. As Hartford drew close, he could make out thin lines of black smoke rising from a fire where the men were branding steers. Hartford glanced over his shoulder and was relieved to see the sheriff wasn't following. Once he had checked what he needed to, he might be able to catch up with him before he reached the main gate.

At the cattle pens, it was just as Hartford suspected. A longhorn was being held down by three guys while a fourth altered the brand. Hartford knew straight off that was what they were doing. Instead of handling a McGreggor brand, the man held a home-made running iron, a length of blackened wood shoved through a saddle cinch ring. He held it over a small fire until the ring glowed and the handle began to smoke, then he traced an addition to the brand that was already there. An LD design became a McG. Concentrating on their work, the men failed to register Hartford's approach until he was right by them.

'Ain't they sent you down with some coffee?' The man doing the branding looked irritated. 'We've been out here all morning.' Clearly in charge, his work clothes were covered in dust and smoke from the fire blackened his face. He looked tired and from what Hartford could see, they weren't even half way through. The stink of burning hide hung in the air.

The other three released the steer which they had had pinned to the ground and jumped back to let him go free. With a strangled grunt and a shake of its head, the terrified animal bucked itself to its feet, flicked its tail and trotted away.

'Why don't you Lazy D guys come down here and help us?' One of the others spoke, a tough cowboy with resentment in his eyes. 'It don't take all of you to sit on the main gate. Up until yesterday, there was only ever one guy on the gate.'

'Yesterday?' Hartford said.

'Yesterday,' the man echoed scornfully. 'When you guys arrived.'

'You going to just sit there on your horse or are you going to get down and give us a hand?' the man doing the branding said.

'Ask me, McGreggor's jumpy all of a sudden,' the second man said. 'Never had more than one guy on the gate before.'

'With this many beeves, who wouldn't be?' A third man spoke. 'Damn hard work branding full-grown steers. Pete got kicked this morning.' He indicated one of the other men.

Pete was younger than the others. Standing back from the group, waiting to be brought into the conversation before he said anything, he smiled when his name was mentioned.

'Might have broke a rib,' Pete said. 'Hurts like hell.'

'Pity you didn't get kicked in the head,' the fourth man said.

'Wouldn't have noticed then, would you?'

The other men laughed. Pete's face reddened, but he stared at a patch of ground down by his feet and smiled again. Teasing like this meant that the older men had accepted him.

'All these come from the Lazy D?' Hartford tried to sound casual. He cast his eye over the pens. There must have been more than seventy beeves between the three pens.

'You brung 'em.' Pete felt confident enough to attempt banter of his own. 'You should know.'

The men all stared at Hartford. They realized something, but hadn't figured out what it was.

'Didn't you?' Pete tried to get someone to laugh at his joke.

Again, none of them laughed.

'How come you don't know that?' The foreman held the running iron at his side. Then he added, 'You come down here to help us or what?'

'Just been with McGreggor,' Hartford said. 'Came down to see how you fellas were getting on.'

'Told you McGreggor was jumpy,' the second man chipped in.

'Shut up, Zac.' Something was making the foreman uneasy.

'We need some of those new guys on the gate to come down here and give us a hand and we need

94

someone to bring us down some coffee.' Zac wouldn't be quiet.

'Maybe Mr McGreggor put the new guys on the gate because they ain't as good as us at doing the real work.' Pete made another play for the approval of the group but everyone ignored him.

There was a shout from further up the track that led towards the main house. A rider careered towards them, his horse kicking up a fierce cloud of dust. As he drew closer, Hartford recognized Logan. When he reached the pens, he jerked his reins and pulled the animal to a standstill.

'You shouldn't be down here,' Logan yelled at Hartford. He looked down distastefully at the dust on his clothes. 'Mr McGreggor told you to leave.' Then he rounded on the foreman. 'What are you doing talking to him anyway?'

'He's one of your guys from the D, ain't he?' The foreman looked baffled.

'Why don't a couple of you fellas come down here and give us a hand?' Zac chimed in. 'It don't take all of you to sit on that gate.'

Hartford turned his horse and started back up the track. Logan shadowed him all the way to the gate. Sheriff Milton was waiting there with Jake Nudd and Clyde Shorter.

'They don't like you guys,' Hartford said. 'They figure you're letting them do all the work.'

Nudd and Shorter looked anxiously at Logan to see if this was true.

'Saw about seventy head with the Lazy D brand,'

Hartford went on. 'You boys cut Dunmore's herd?'

'Don't know what you're talking about,' Logan said innocently. 'Mr McGreggor took us on to guard his gate. We don't have nothing to do with the herd.'

NINE

After leaving the McGreggor spread, Sheriff Milton insisted on heading out to Snake's Creek.

'Ought to see where it was done,' he said.

On the ride, the sheriff became lost in his own thoughts. When Hartford tried to tell him how he had witnessed McGreggor's men doctoring the brands on Lazy D steers, the sheriff merely nodded as if he already knew.

Hartford hadn't visited Snake's Creek since he was a boy. His mind played over old memories of his pa taking him out there. What a hero his pa had seemed then. Tall and strong, there seemed nothing he couldn't fix, no question he couldn't answer and nothing he didn't know. He taught him patience and carefulness, the right way to cast a line, how to use the home-made net to land his catch without harming it. Pa always brought Boone along too and set him up with a pole just like Hartford's.

But it was never long before Boone became bored. His mood darkened, he complained about the heat and threw stones in the creek. The older he got, the more readily he found excuses to head into town instead, usually on the pretext of running some errand or other. Then he would stay there all day, hang around the livery stable or the saloon and arrive back home after dark, sometimes after his pa had gone looking for him, full of stories of stand-offs and fist fights between the cattlemen. To shock his ma, he made a point of using language he picked up during the course of the day, which had never been heard at home.

Joe Hartford taught his sons all he knew about the farm, how to dig wells and turn parched land into productive fields, how to shear sheep, raise hogs and milk the cow; each spring they witnessed the birth of lambs. While the boys were young, their parents were happy, the farm prospered and everything was fine.

From the get-go everyone acknowledged that Boone was a difficult kid. Tantrums and disobedience, which could be excused while he was a child, became serious when he didn't grow out of them as a teenager. When he told his parents he hated the farm, everything they had worked for, it broke their hearts. The constant strain of being peacemaker and worrying about what Boone was up to, on top of the toll of gruelling farm work, wore his mother out.

Joe Hartford barely noticed. He buried himself in his work. Somehow, far away from the house, there were always fences that needed mending and livestock that had strayed, which meant he arrived home after dark, too late to do anything but eat and go straight to bed. He didn't want to have to deal with Boone or listen to his wife's complaints about how rude or lazy he had been that day or how she had failed to get him to do his chores. Joe Hartford's dream of handing on a thriving farm to his two sons was broken. He began to realize that the assumptions he had made about how the future would turn out were simply wrong.

To help him get through all this, Joe Hartford regularly took refuge in a bottle of red eye in the evenings. Not being an argumentative man, his drinking never led to fights and he was never so much as discourteous to his wife. It was simply a way to prevent himself thinking about problems he knew he could never solve, his wife's failing health, Boone's apparent loathing of everything he stood for and the fact that Hartford's ambition to become a Pinkerton Agent meant that he too would turn his back on the farm.

When they reached Snake's Creek, Hartford and the sheriff edged their horses along the narrow track which zig-zagged down to the river. The high sides of the creek provided welcome shade. As Hartford and the sheriff rounded a bend, they saw a figure hunched over a fishing pole. Pops Wardell.

'Figured no one would mind, now that . . . I mean . . . Dunmore being . . .' The old man didn't notice them approach until they were right on top of him. He jumped up and knocked his pole off the rock where it was balanced.

'That's fine Pops,' the sheriff assured him. 'Come

to look at where it happened.'

'I can help you there, Sheriff.' Pops Wardell scrambled up from the river's edge on to the path.

The next bend upstream was a place where animals came to drink. The flow of the river slowed here and the water's edge was shallow.

'Right here.' Pops stood still and pointed.

Hartford noticed animal tracks, hoof prints and some human boot prints. He climbed down off his horse and inspected the dirt. Amidst the confusion of tracks, he could just make out parallel lines made by wheels.

'Bill Greely bring a wagon out here when he came to pick up the body?'

'No sir,' Pops said. 'Said he wouldn't be able to get it close enough to the river. Led a mule out from the stable, carried him back to town on that.'

Pops gave them a thorough tour of the site, pointing out tracks and places where he had seen tracks which were now covered over. Hartford examined the ground, but the dirt was so dry, the slightest breeze could make hoof prints disappear almost as soon as they had been made. He kept his eyes peeled for anything else, clothing snagged on a thorn, a shell casing perhaps, but found nothing. The hoof prints Pops swore he had seen heading south had disappeared too.

'What d'you reckon about the tracks?' Pops was excited. He wanted to be a part of the investigation. 'See, I reckon Dunmore came out here looking for me. He knew I wasn't going to quit fishing just on his say so.' Pops drew himself up to his full height. 'We were playing a game of cat and mouse.'

On the way back to town, Hartford insisted on describing the brands he had seen being altered on the McGreggor ranch.

'Same thing on every ranch in Texas.' The sheriff was unimpressed. 'If you ask me, that's why the bosses keep the cowpokes' wages so low. The only guys who miss out are the ones who do the rustling. They all think they're going to make enough money to put down a payment on a spread of their own. Never happens.' The sheriff suddenly became serious. 'Bet you any money you like Logan and the others will have sold the beeves to McGreggor at a rock bottom price. All they'll have made will be enough for a couple of nights drinking at Pearl's place. When they sobered up and went asking McGreggor for work, he'll have said he'd take them on as a favour because Dunmore fired them. Then he'll pay them even less than Dunmore did.'

Riding side by side, the men pulled their hats down low. The hard midday light stabbed their eyes and the heat lashed their shoulders. Sweat ran down their temples and cut tracks in the dust that clung to their faces. Neither of them spoke for a while. Their bodies relaxed into the regular, monotonous pace of their horses.

Sheriff Milton slipped into a reverie, a place where intuition, instinct and experience met and combined into thought. When he was walking, he grimaced with pain at every step, but here in the saddle, his face was relaxed, content. It was at least two miles before he broke his silence.

'Don't think I've forgotten about the jail break.' The sheriff raised his chin as he turned to Hartford so that the shadow cast by his hat did not hide the look of determination on his face.

'Has it always been like this between McGreggor and Dunmore?' Hartford wanted the sheriff to focus on Dunmore again. Some cowhand busting out of jail didn't seem important.

'Forever,' the sheriff said. 'McGreggor arrived down here when land was free for the taking. Following year, Dunmore turned up and lay claim to his spread. Any parcels of land they couldn't sign for legally they grabbed anyway. Always argued over that boundary of theirs, I doubt if either of them knows where the true line runs.'

A couple of miles up ahead, the wooden buildings which made up the town shimmered in the heat. From here, they seemed part of the landscape. The bleached cottonwood was the same smoky grey as the caliche dust around it, cast the same pools of black shadow as the cactus plants which grew outside it, and sat as still as the rocks strewn along the desert trail.

Hartford remembered the excitement he felt as a boy whenever he witnessed the men working on a new building, the sound of their hammers pealing like bells out across the empty plain and the sight of the newly cut wood, as pale as early sunshine. Now, the town was not so much growing out of the land-scape as sinking back into it. His memory was of a place of hope nourished by dreams of the future; now it was a place of despair where old enmities were laid bare.

'Dunmore called in the Pinkerton Agency because McGreggor was getting the upper hand,' Hartford said. In his head, pieces fell into place. 'Allan Pinkerton thought he was answering the cry for help from a cattleman terrorised by a gang of rustlers. He had no idea he was joining one side in a range war.'

As they entered the town, the doors to the livery were open. Inside, Bill Greely was measuring coffin length planks of pine. The dirt floor around him was littered with yellow shavings and the smell of planed wood sweetened the air. Greely looked up and smiled his black smile as Hartford and the sheriff rode past.

At the saloon, Pearl was adding rosettes to the loops of bunting which ran the length of the porch. There were more rosettes and twists of crepe paper along the lintel. On the doors, the names Boone and Mary May were picked out in paper flowers.

'What do you think?' Pearl was pleased with her handiwork. 'I'm guessing the wedding's still at one o'clock tomorrow. Nobody's told me it ain't.'

TEN

The saloon was empty. The tables and chairs were neatly arranged down the centre of the room, paper streamers looped between the rafters and white paper rosettes were hung at intervals along the walls. The oak top of the bar was polished to a shine and the shelves behind it were stacked with clean glasses. Even Pearl's twelve-gauge which lay on top of the bar had been given a once over. Hartford hung his gun behind the door.

'Saloon's closed until tomorrow.' Pearl was excited. 'Want to get everything right. It ain't every day we have a wedding breakfast in here.'

'All prepared with a scattergun on the bar?' Hartford teased her.

'Never know what kind of mood everyone will be in.' There was a serious look in her eyes.

'Seen Boone?' Hartford said.

'Not for a few days.' Pearl reached under the bar for a bottle of red eye and a glass. 'He called in last weekend with Mary May.'

104

'Mary May is out at the McGreggor place,' Hartford said. 'No sign of Boone.'

Pearl poured the whiskey and pushed the glass over to Hartford.

'Done the place up real nice,' Hartford could see the effort she had put in.

'You think this wedding will be going ahead?' Pearl came straight out with it. 'In view of ...' Her voice trailed as she cast her eye over the line of rosettes along the walls and the streamers overhead. All that work. 'There was always fireworks between Mary May and her pa,' Pearl went on. 'When she came in to town, she used to sneak in here through the back way in case someone saw her. She was always full of stories about how Dunmore wouldn't let her go anywhere, just wanted her to keep in the ranch house all the time and how sick she was of it. She said the Lazy D was a prison, she'd do anything to escape if she could think of a way. I felt sorry for her. She's a sweet kid.' Pearl reached under the bar, brought out a glass and poured a slug of red eye for herself. 'Then along came Boone.'

'The more Dunmore tried to prise Mary May and Boone apart, the more they stuck together,' Hartford said. 'He came out to the farm yesterday to try to take her home.'

'Worked out why we've got the no gun rule in here?' Pearl didn't wait for him to answer. 'Couple of months ago, Boone rolls in all liquored up, demanding a bottle of red eye. I suggested to him that he should just relax and head home. He pulls out his .45

and starts shooting the place up. See those holes up there?' Pearl pointed to a line of six unevenly spaced bullet holes in the pitch of the roof which Hartford hadn't noticed before. 'Sheriff took Boone's gun away and slung him in a cell till he sobered up.'

Hartford sipped his red eye and felt his throat burn. Boone was born with a scowl on his face, their ma used to say. If things were as he wanted, everything was fine. Any problems, he got angry. If anyone stood in his way, there was trouble.

'Boone went to Dunmore, trying to do the right thing, just like Charlie Nudd had. Pretty much got the same reaction. Only this time, Mary May joined in too. Told her pa that she had been courting Boone in secret and they were planning to get hitched whether he agreed or not. Well, that was too much for old man Dunmore. He got Charlie to fling Boone off the Lazy D, which Charlie was only too happy to do. Dunmore said if Boone showed his face on Lazy D land again, he'd shoot him himself.'

Pearl shook her head sadly.

'The more Mary May pleaded with old man Dunmore, the more he took against Boone. Said it was bad enough Boone being a sodbuster's son, but no daughter of his was going to marry a good-for-nothing who had abandoned his pa's farm to work on a construction site in Dallas.'

Pearl looked quickly at Hartford. Talking about his family like this, maybe she had said too much.

'It's OK,' Hartford saw the concern in her eyes. 'Boone is Boone.'

'Must earn good money up in Dallas,' Pearl said. 'Drinks all round every time he comes in here.'

Hartford pictured Annie in her threadbare house dress, the broken fences and the termite dust on the porch.

The saloon doors opened and made them both look up. A slim figure stood there, a woman, hesitating on whether or not to come in.

'We're closed,' Pearl called before she realized who it was.

The woman stood just inside the door, unable to take another step as if some kind of exhaustion locked her limbs. A cloud of misery shrouded her. Her eyes pleaded with them, but she was silent; no words would form in her mouth. She swayed slightly and for a moment it looked as if she might topple over where she stood. Hartford jumped down off his barstool and ran towards her, arms outstretched.

'Annie,' Hartford's voice came from somewhere in his chest, hoarse and breathless. In his haste, he knocked over his stool with a crash and his footsteps clattered on the wooden floor. He flung his arms round his sister's slim shoulders and held her tight. Tears bathed her face. Apart from her livid eyelids, her face was bone white. After a second, she summoned her strength. 'It's Pa. I just left him on the porch and went inside for a moment. I was going to get him something to eat. I heard him coughing, like he always does. I didn't think anything of it, I mean. . . .'

She broke off from talking, a sob rose in her chest and knocked the breath out of her. Hartford reached out to take her arm but she shook him off, determined to deliver her terrible message.

'Pa's dead, Hart.'

As Hartford held his sister, his legs felt weak and pain twisted in his gut. In his head, images of his pa from their meeting yesterday blurred with memories from years ago, the two of them fishing up on the Blue River, him helping his pa to hoe weeds in the vegetable patch and his pa laughing because the hoe was taller than he was, the old man bent almost double in his rocking chair, breath clawing in his chest, hating the world and everyone in it.

Hartford felt Pearl's arm across his shoulders. She embraced them both and for some immeasurable length of time they all stood locked together in the empty saloon. Golden dust motes danced around them in the thin beams of sunlight that fell through the holes in the roof.

Eventually, though none of them could have said how long they stood there, Pearl let go. Making her way back to the bar, her hand touched the backs of the chairs she passed as if she needed the fleeting support of each one to help her walk the length of the saloon. She righted the stool Hartford had kicked over and poured a red eye for Annie.

'Where's Boone?' Annie looked around at the empty chairs as if she was expecting to see him.

'Ain't here.'

'I thought he would be with you.' Pearl and Hartford answered at the same time, their words criss-crossing.

'I reckoned, tonight being the last night before his wedding. . . .' Annie looked from one to the other.

Pearl pushed the red eye along the bar towards Annie, but she shook her head.

'Well, where is he?' She stared round the place again and for the first time seemed to notice the streamers which ran the length of the room.

Hartford didn't know what to say. Had Boone run off somewhere? What had he done? Was he hiding out? When Pearl caught his eye, he changed the subject.

'I should take you back to the farm.' Hartford looked at Annie, her dishevelled hair, bleached face. Her strength, her ability to cope, even her capacity to think in her usual practical way, had all deserted her. She had become a version of herself he had never seen before, helpless and lost.

'Maybe he's with Mary May.' Annie struggled to put her thoughts into some kind of order.

'Mary May's out at the McGreggor place,' Hartford said gently. 'Boone ain't there.'

Annie nodded, but Hartford wasn't sure that she had taken in what he said.

'I'll tell Bill Greely.' Pearl wanted to do something practical. 'He'll take care of . . .' Her words were lost as she hurried out of the saloon.

Outside, there was no breeze to relieve the remains of the stifling afternoon heat which weighed in the air. Colour sank back into everything. The dirt underfoot was no longer white, the grain was visible in the planks of the wooden buildings, the arching sky, which had been pale for hours, was a dusty blue. As usual, the street outside the saloon was empty. Hartford insisted on helping Annie up into her saddle and climbed up on to his appaloosa.

Beside the saloon, a covered wagon was parked up. From inside came the gentle, rhythmic sound of someone snoring. The back board was down and they could see the two upturned soles of a man's boots as he lay stretched out. Hartford noticed a smile touch the corner of Annie's mouth.

'The preacher,' Hartford explained. 'For tomorrow.'

Sheriff Milton emerged from his office and strode across the street towards them. Each step made him wince with pain, but he refused to slow his pace.

'Pearl just told me.' Not knowing what else to do, he took off his hat and turned the brim nervously in his hands. 'Your pa and me, we go way back. Last few years were hard on him, but it wasn't always like that.' He reached up and squeezed Annie's hand. 'You did everything you could and he loved you for it.'

'Thank you, Sheriff,' Annie managed a tight smile.

At the far end of the street, the sight of Bill Greely emerging from the livery made Annie catch her breath. She couldn't take her eyes off him as he made his way towards them.

'Do you know where Boone is, Sheriff?' Annie sounded helpless again.

'I'm sorry, Annie.' The sheriff shook his head. 'We'll find him for you.'

The sheriff read the disappointment in Annie's

face. He didn't want to leave her with some empty platitude.

'You know what Boone's like, Annie. He goes where he wants to go. But I'd lay good money he'll be here tomorrow.' The sheriff nodded towards the saloon.

A streamer which Pearl had fastened to the front of the porch had come adrift and trailed on the ground. A white paper rosette lay in the dirt by the saloon steps.

ELEVEN

Dog eat dog. That was life in this part of Texas since the first wagon rolled in.

As he rode back into town early the following morning, Hartford was in a black mood. The state of the family farm depressed him. He reflected on the number of people who came out here with hopes sky-high only to have them dashed. Some fell prey to saloon card sharps and lost their fortunes before they had made them; others managed to buy land but became victims of drought, or their stock became diseased and died; still more simply never turned a profit before the banks called in their loans. Hartford had seen families abandon their farms, sell them at a loss and flee. He had seen stores open in town, trade for a while and then shut down. And this was even before barriers went up on the Shawnee Trail.

There were always vultures circling. When a business closed in town, a buyer would appear just at the right time and snap it up at a bargain price. When word got around that the bank was about to foreclose on a farm, a neighbour would put in a derisory offer and because the vendor had nowhere else to turn, it would be accepted. According to Sheriff Milton, cattle rustling was almost a local sport. If you managed to seize hold of something in this unforgiving land, there would be someone ready to snatch it out of your grasp the first chance they got.

Even before Hartford had packed his bag and headed off for Chicago, life here was hard. But back then there was a spirit in the place; it was a wide open land and everyone had a chance. Now, the town was in a sorry state. Pearl was guarding what was left of her pa's once thriving saloon with a twelve-gauge. The sheriff was about to retire and no one had come forward to take his place. The most activity Hartford had seen on the main street was Bill Greely building a coffin.

Hartford's thoughts continued to wander. The town might be dying, but the ranches were still doing well. The Lazy D was thriving despite whatever rustling had been going on until Dunmore got shot. Instincts for a bargain still sharp, Dunmore had even put in a sly offer for the Hartford farm when he saw what condition it was in. Even his pa had managed to keep the farm going until he got sick. But the real winner was McGreggor. Hartford couldn't get the image of the whitewashed walls and the luxurious green lawn out of his head. He had never seen a place like it.

Sheriff Milton was sitting on a chair on the porch

outside his office when Hartford reached town.

'Didn't bring Annie with you?'

'Wanted time on her own before she rode into town for all this.' Hartford gestured towards the bunting which decorated the saloon.

'One of a kind, your sister.' The sheriff shook his head. 'Living with your pa ain't been easy.'

Hartford dismounted and tethered his horse to the rail.

'Boone show up?' the sheriff went on.

Hartford shook his head.

'By the way, a rider brought a message from Fort Worth. The Pinkerton Office in Chicago wired to say you'll be arriving any day.' Sheriff Milton smiled at his own joke. 'They put up two thousand miles of wire to tell you something you already know. Modern world makes me feel old.' The sheriff grimaced as he straightened his legs in front of him. 'Damn knees. You think Boone might have headed back to Dallas?' The sheriff slipped the question in quickly while Hartford was still amused at the idea of the out-of-date wire arriving.

It was something which had occurred to Hartford, but he had dismissed it out of hand. Now, the sheriff coming up with the same idea made him think.

'Supposed to be his wedding day, why would he do that?'

Hartford could read Sheriff Milton well enough by now to know that he had something on his mind, which for the moment he intended to keep to himself.

'All we can do is wait for him to turn up.'

Hartford had agreed with Annie that he would settle up with Bill Greely. When he got down to the livery, Greely was sweeping up. A new pine coffin lay across a pair of saw horses and lengths of pine were cut ready for another. Wood shavings littered the floor and the air smelled of sawdust.

'Your pa was a good man, always looked out for his own. I knew him a long time.' Bill Greely leaned on his yard broom. A kindly smile showed his black teeth. 'Won't be no charge for his pine box.'

Hartford turned to go. It was at this point that people usually started to tell him stories about good times they had spent with his pa in the past. But right now, he wasn't in the mood. Everything weighed on him. He was worried about Annie, on her own at the farm; if she hadn't been adamant, he would never have left her alone this morning. He still couldn't figure out what Mary May was doing with McGreggor. He was no closer to catching Dunmore's killer. The wedding was due to take place in a few hours and Boone was God knows where.

'Lucky there's a preacher in town,' Greely called after him. 'Burials are always better if you've got a preacher.'

Hartford started down the street towards the saloon. After a few paces he stopped abruptly, little clouds of dust exploding round his boots.

'Any idea where Boone is?' He turned back to Greely who had started sweeping again. 'You keep his horse in there, don't you?'

'Dallas.' Greely looked up from his broom. 'Took his horse Friday afternoon. Flew in here like the devil was on his tail. Said something about business he had to finish and he'd be back in time to get hitched.'

On his way up the street, the thought echoed in Hartford's head. What was so urgent Boone had to abandon his fiancée and high-tail it to a construction site in Dallas two days before he was due to get wed?

The atmosphere in the saloon was rich with the smell of fresh ground coffee. Hartford found the preacher having breakfast alone. He was sitting at a table with a coffee pot and a plate of beans in front of him.

'Good morning, friend.' He waved Hartford over as soon as he entered.

The preacher was short and round-faced with straw-coloured hair.

There were dark pouches under his eyes, his eyelids looked sore and his face carried a few days growth of yellow stubble. His waistcoat was tight over his stomach and a battered black hat was planted firmly on his head.

'Care to join me? I'm sure Miss Pearl will provide us with a second cup,' he grinned broadly. There was something in his manner which said that no matter what, he always woke up with a smile on his face.

Pearl came out from behind the bar and slammed a second cup down on the preacher's table.

'I've taken the Reverend's bottle away from him,' she declared loudly. 'Told him no red eye until after the ceremony.'

116

'You see, Miss Pearl has all our best interests at heart.' Determined to see the good in every situation, the preacher beamed.

'This is Hart, brother to the groom,' Pearl said curtly. 'Now drink that coffee and eat something.'

The preacher poured a cup of oily coffee for Hart.

'Miss Pearl makes her coffee mighty strong,' he confided after Pearl had retreated behind the bar. As he picked up a fork and started to attack the beans, the smile slid from his face.

Between mouthfuls, the preacher recommended a certain pick-me-up which often came in useful in the mornings. He happened to have a case in his wagon, he said, and could let Hartford have a bottle cut-price. It operated as a cure-all. Not only did it give you a lift first thing in the morning, it kept out the cold and was good for rheumatism, arthritis, gout and all manner of stomach complaints. When he looked up and discovered Pearl was still watching him, he lifted his coffee cup in her direction and let her see him take a slug.

Hartford told the preacher about his pa.

'Another funeral?' He gave Hartford a professional beam. 'I should be happy to say a few words.'

The wedding ceremony was to take place on the empty ground beside the saloon where the preacher's wagon was parked. The guests would be a tempting captive audience and Hartford wondered how soon it would be before the Reverend began a sales pitch for his cure-all. He knocked back his coffee, firmly declined to purchase a bottle of the preacher's elixir and set off across the street to the sheriff's office.

The thought that he and his pa had not spoken kindly during their last conversation weighed on Hartford. He tried to comfort himself with the thought that at least he had been in town when the old man passed on. At least he had seen him one last time, even if they hadn't been able to make peace. Hartford shaded his eyes and peered the length of the street in the direction he knew Annie would come. Greely's hammering kept up a gentle percussion at the far end of town.

Sheriff Milton insisted that he had paperwork to attend to and pointed Hartford towards a chair on the office porch, which gave him a perfect view of the saloon. As the morning progressed, people came and went. Pearl supervised a procession of townsfolk carrying baskets and plates loaded with provisions. Pops Wardell turned up in a clean shirt, sat down in his usual chair outside the saloon door and promptly dozed off. Eventually Bill Greely stopped hammering and sauntered up the street, waved at Hartford and grinned his black-toothed grin. It began to feel like all the bunting on the saloon meant something and there was going to be a celebration after all. Even so, whenever Hartford called to the sheriff to come and join him, he refused to come out on to the porch, insisting he still had paperwork to get through – even though he wouldn't say what it was.

A gang of hands from the McGreggor ranch arrived. Logan, Jake Nudd and Clyde Shorter were with them and studiously avoided looking towards the sheriff's office. Charlie Nudd and guys from the Lazy D, all spruced up with clean clothes and new kerchiefs round their necks followed close behind. McGreggor and Mary May rode in together.

Mary May's face was washed out and joyless, her hair was in a loose plait down her back and she was wearing the clothes Hartford had seen her in at McGreggor's the previous day. McGreggor himself looked stern and kept close to her as if anyone who wanted to speak to her had to go through him first. It was almost as if he had decided to bring his men with him in case of trouble. Mary May would have made some arrangement with Pearl to get changed in a room at the back of the saloon, Hartford assumed. But something wasn't right. For a start, there was no buggy. Why had McGreggor let her ride a pony to her own wedding?

Hartford watched them all dismount outside the saloon. McGreggor waved the men to go inside ahead of him and he caught Mary May's arm to hold her back. They were too far away for Hartford to hear what they were saying, but McGreggor seemed to be insisting on something. He kept hold of her elbow, even when she tried to pull away. He looked severe, an angry parent lecturing a child. Close to tears, Mary May shook her head violently. Whatever it was he wanted her to do, she was putting her foot down.

McGreggor looked up and down the street. Keeping an eye out for someone? Looking to see if anyone was within earshot and could overhear them?

Who knew? At that moment, the sheriff emerged from his office. The movement across the street caught McGreggor's attention for a moment, Mary May pulled away and ran up the steps into the saloon leaving him calling after her. Taking time to collect himself, McGreggor checked the reins of the horses tethered to the hitching rail and, after another glance up and down the street, followed her into the saloon.

'Something's not right,' Hartford said. 'Boone ain't even here.'

'He ain't late yet.' The sheriff pulled out a steel watch from his vest pocket.

He pulled up a chair opposite Hartford, felt for his tobacco pouch and began to roll a cigarette.

'Reason you were sent down here in the first place kinda got lost with everything that's gone on.'

It sounded like a simple observation, but the sheriff was building up to something. Hartford could feel it.

'The rustling. I saw them changing the Lazy D brand out at McGreggor's,' Hartford said. 'As soon as we make the arrests, I'll contact Chicago.'

'Reckon you know who's behind it?'

The question took Hartford by surprise.

'I told you. I saw McGreggor's men changing the Lazy D brands with my own eyes. McGreggor got Logan and his bunch to cut Dunmore's herd and when Dunmore found out and fired them, McGreggor took them on.'

The sheriff knew all this, so why was he asking?

'The rider from Fort Worth bought two wires.

120

Modern technology catching up with itself. I let you see the first one while I had a think about the second.' The sheriff finished rolling his cigarette and patted his pockets in search of a match. He eventually tracked one down in the breast pocket of his shirt, flicked the head with his thumbnail and watched it splutter alight. He took a deep draw and the heady tobacco scent filled the morning air.

'Telling you I'm on my way?' Hartford expected a joke, but the sheriff was serious.

'Reading between the lines, it says you're on the wrong trail.'

Looking at Hartford closely, the sheriff drew out a folded telegraph paper from his vest pocket and handed it over.

Hartford felt a chill pass through him, even though the heat of the day was in the air. There was the sound of voices and laughter over at the saloon, but it seemed far away. He unfolded the paper. It was a wire from the Pinkerton Office in Chicago addressed to Sheriff Milton, Credence via Commanding Officer Fort Worth.

RINGLEADER LAZY D RUSTLING IDENTI-
FIED STOP EVIDENCE ABILENE AGENT
STOP INSTRUCT AGENT ARREST BOONE
HARTFORD STOP WITHOUT DELAY STOP
ALLAN PINKERTON.

Hartford felt like someone had punched him in the gut.

Without taking his eyes off Hartford, the sheriff sat back in his chair, straightened his legs in front of him and took another draw from his cigarette.

'Boone had been rustling Dunmore's beeves. Dunmore tumbled to it and called in the Pinkertons. Sure gives Boone a motive for killing Dunmore, don't it?'

TWELVE

An hour later, Hartford gave up. If Boone wasn't here by now he was never going to show. With one last glance towards the edge of town, he left the sheriff rolling himself another cigarette and crossed the street to the saloon. He had to speak to Mary May. If she didn't at least have a suspicion about Boone's whereabouts, then no one had. The sun was high and just stepping out from under the protection of the porch meant he felt the heat across his shoulders like a brand.

By the time he reached the middle of the street, Hartford could hear raised voices coming from the saloon, a man and a woman. The man was stubborn, at the end of reasonableness and laying down the law. The woman was tearful, hurt and refused to be pushed around. McGreggor and Mary May.

Hartford stopped inside the saloon door to let his eyes get accustomed to the shadows. Before he could see properly, Pearl was at his side demanding to know where Boone was.

'He's putting the poor girl through hell.' She was righteous with anger.

As Hartford's vision returned, he could see groups of people sitting round tables. None of them was drinking. A line of gun belts hung by the door. Logan and the men from McGreggor's place huddled in the shadows in one corner, with Jake Nudd trying to make himself invisible at the back of the group. Bill Greely and Pops Wardell sat far away from them at the opposite end of the room. Next to them were three guys, clearly self-conscious in their best clothes, who Hartford recognized as hands from the Lazy D. Then there was the family who ran the store occupying another table and alongside them, folks from the outlying farms. Everyone was sitting in shocked silence, nervously watching an argument between McGreggor and Mary May come to the boil. Pearl hovered close, like a referee who might have to step in at any moment.

Mary May stood sobbing with grief, anger and stubbornness. Torn streamers and bunting lay strewn at her feet and in her hand she gripped a white rosette she had just ripped off the front of the bar. McGreggor was close beside her. Each time he made a grab for her arm she pulled away.

'I told you you should have stayed at the ranch and let me handle this.' McGreggor spoke too loud. He was not used to being defied. His voice was strained with sympathy wearing thin.

'I have to wait for Boone,' Mary May sobbed. 'I will not leave. I want him to hear it from me first.'

124

'Hon . . .' Pearl tried to plead with her, but Mary May turned away.

'He will come.' Mary May screwed up the rosette in her fist and threw it down on to the floor. 'I know he will.'

At the sound of footsteps on the porch, everyone turned towards the door. Annie came in wearing her best house dress and a straw bonnet. She stood beside Hartford, blinking to let her eyes adjust.

'Do you know where Boone is?' Mary May catapulted herself towards her friend. Annie seized her, hugged her close and after a moment led her towards an empty table. She grabbed Hartford's sleeve with her other hand and pulled him with them.

'Damnit, open the bar, Pearl,' McGreggor commanded. 'Everyone needs a shot of red eye.'

Shouts of agreement chorused from all round the room.

'One shot.' Pearl glared at the preacher. 'There's still half an hour to go before the ceremony's due to start.'

The tension in the air evaporated as soon as Pearl poured the red eye. McGreggor and Charlie Nudd took it upon themselves to carry trays of whiskey from table to table. Everyone started to smile and talk and take care not to stare at Mary May. They avoided commenting on the fact that she wasn't even wearing her best clothes, let alone a wedding dress, or that there was no sign of the groom.

The loss of both the young women's fathers coinciding with the wedding was almost too much for the

townsfolk to take in. Many of them had known Mary
May and Annie since they had been children and if
sitting quietly and waiting to see how things turned
out was the kind of support the girls needed right
now, then that was what they would give them.

Annie sat with one arm across Mary May's shoulder while holding on to Hartford's arm with her
other hand.

'You ain't seen Boone for two days? Not since you
left the farm?'

Hartford pictured them galloping out of the yard,
their mouths full of laughter, Mary May's hair flying
behind her in the wind.

'I told you. I told Mr McGreggor.' Mary May's tearstained face was pale. 'Why do you keep asking?'

'After you left the farm. . . ?'

'Boone said he had to get back to work.' Mary May
sounded weary.

'So since Friday, Boone has been up in Dallas?'
Hartford felt Annie squeeze his arm, warning him.
'Could he have come back yesterday, maybe?'

'You mean without me knowing?' It took a
moment for Mary May to grasp what he was driving
at. She pushed Annie's arm off her shoulder. Her
face froze. 'To do what? To kill my pa? Take him out
to Snake's Creek and put a bullet in him?' Panic rose
up in her and she turned to Annie. 'Is that what you
think too?'

'Of course not,' Annie tried to reassure her. 'Hart
doesn't mean anything by it. He's just a law man
asking questions.'

'Have you asked anyone else where they were?' Mary May met Hartford head on. 'Or is it just Boone you're after? What about me? I could have shot my pa, couldn't I? Led him out there and put a bullet in him.'

Her tears broke again and cascaded down her cheeks. She let Annie pull her close as if she didn't have the strength left to resist.

'Boone isn't a bad guy,' she said quietly. 'He gets bored easily that's all. He wants excitement. That's why he can't stand being on the farm day after day.'

'You aren't going to marry him, are you?' Annie saw it now. 'That's why you came here today to tell him. That's why you won't let McGreggor take you home.'

'I'm sorry, Annie,' Mary May turned to her friend. 'We were playing a game, having fun. My pa was riled and that made it even more crazy for us. Who doesn't want some craziness? We never really meant it.

'Then one day Boone announces he's been to see Pearl, told her to decorate the saloon and get hold of a preacher. That sent my pa into a frenzy. Said he'd rather shoot the pair of us rather than see us hitched.'

Her words melted away as she spoke them. In her face was the realization that what Hartford had hinted at could be true.

'Now come on. Boone could never do something like that.' Annie fondly squeezed her shoulder, but her kind words rang hollow.

The look Mary May gave Hartford said yes he could.

'Lots of people. . . .' Annie stumbled through what she was trying to say. 'I mean, anyone who owns a spread out here makes enemies. That's just how it is. I'm telling you, Boone didn't have it in him. You know that. There's always rustlers about. It could have been anyone.'

'I think you should wait here for Boone.' Hartford took charge. 'I think you should tell these people there'll be no wedding and let them go home.'

How typical it was of Boone to make harum-scarum wedding plans which left the whole town in the lurch. How typical of Annie to make excuses for him. On the other hand, even though Mary May was weighed down with grief for her pa, she thought enough of Boone to come here to face him today.

'If Boone isn't here by one o'clock, I'll tell them.' Mary May got to her feet. Her face was pale and determined. She avoided catching the eye of any of them.

'Fifteen minutes,' Annie said. They all looked up at the clock behind the bar.

Mary May crossed the room as if nothing was wrong, smiled politely at people she knew, avoided McGreggor and sat herself down beside the preacher. At the same time, McGreggor strode the length of the saloon until he came face to face with Hartford.

'You been putting ideas in that poor girl's head?' Irritation burned in his face. 'She should be coming home with me. That brother of yours has let her down.'

'Outside,' Hartford snapped. He jumped to his feet, seized McGreggor's arm and pulled him towards the door.

Across the street Sheriff Milton was still sitting on his porch. As Hartford looked, he pulled out his pocket watch to check the time.

'If you've got something to say to me, then say it.' McGreggor shook himself free of Hartford's grasp.

'Heard you made an offer on the Lazy D,' Hartford said flatly.

'Who told you that?' McGreggor rounded on him.

'Know for a fact that you've been cutting Dunmore's herd.'

'What?' McGreggor saw immediately where this was going.

'That wouldn't make Dunmore a friend of yours, now would it?'

Hartford was determined to get an answer out of McGreggor one way or another.

Hartford was well aware that his pa had lived all his life in the shadow of the Lazy D and the McGreggor spread, vast ranches which occupied square mile after square mile. All his life he struggled to make a living on his hundred and fifty acres. His wife died, he endured the war and his health gave out. His sons were no good to him, one left home and the other let the farm decay.

Dunmore could have helped Joe Hartford, but instead he waited until the farm was doomed and then offered to buy him out. McGreggor could have been a good neighbour to Dunmore but instead he shifted the boundary and rustled his cattle. Now McGreggor stood right in front of Hartford, never for a second doubting that his wealth give him every right to be in charge. Hartford fought back the desire to lash out, to dispense with justice, to blame McGreggor for everything. Then out of the corner of his eye, he noticed some movement across the street and he suddenly became aware of the sheriff watching him.

'Are you accusing me of something?' McGreggor said sharply.

'I saw your men changing the Lazy D brand with my own eyes.' Hartford stood his ground.

McGreggor's laugh was mocking and humourless.

'Better sit down while I explain something to you, son.' He gestured towards a hard chair and took Pops' wicker for himself. 'Those beeves were mine. My men reclaimed them. Dunmore altered my brand, I changed it back. Come out to the ranch and take a look if you want.'

'*Same thing on every ranch in Texas. If you ask me that's why the bosses keep the cowpokes' wages so low*' Hartford remembered the sheriff's words.

McGreggor leaned forward in his chair, rested his arms on his knees and opened his hands as if he was making Hartford a gift of something.

'Think about it. Why would I need to steal seventy longhorns from the Lazy D? There's more than a thousand head on my place right now.'

'Those men on your gate, Logan and the others, they're the guys who did the rustling,' Hartford persisted. 'Sheriff threw Charlie Nudd's brother in jail.'

McGreggor's brittle laugh sounded like a cough. 'When you've known Sheriff Milton as long as I have, you'll understand that the first thing he does is keep the peace. He takes the heat out of things and sorts out the rights and wrongs later. Anyway, Jake Nudd ain't at all like his brother, a night in the lock-up probably did him some good.'

McGreggor sat back in his chair and stared at Hartford as if he was trying to figure something out.

'Those guys on your gate . . .' Hartford tried again.

'Trust them as far as I could spit,' McGreggor said. 'Keeping 'em on the gate makes them feel important and it keeps them out of harm's way. Never let them near my herd. Whenever Dunmore's guys stole a few head of mine, I used Logan and the others to get them back.'

'You moved the boundary fence into Lazy D land.' Hartford didn't give up.

'Same deal.' The wicker chair creaked as McGreggor shifted his weight. Unused to being challenged, the effort of holding on to his temper showed in his face.

'We've argued over that boundary line for years. Dunmore threatened to report me to the Pinkertons, so I reckoned it was about time I settled the boundary once and for all.'

From inside the saloon, they could hear Mary May's voice, though not clearly enough to make out what she was saying. Across the street, the sheriff ground out the end of his cigarette under his boot heel and checked his watch again. It must be one o'clock.

The mid-day sunlight bounced off the sandy street, shadows as black as pitch nestled under the porches of the cottonwood buildings. The air was dry and smelled of dust. Heat pressed down on the day. Satisfied that he had got the better of all Hartford's questions, a narrow smile played on McGreggor's mouth. Across the street, the sheriff stood up and stared out into the empty prairie.

'Dunmore was found killed out at Snake's Creek.' Hartford spoke quietly so McGreggor had to lean forward to catch what he was saying.

'Pops Wardell was fishing out there and found his body in the reeds.'

'So what?' McGreggor stared at him.

'Where were you Friday afternoon?'

'Damnit to hell, boy.' McGreggor jumped up as if Hartford had touched him with a branding iron. 'I've taken the time to explain everything and you still don't get how things are. You started out a sod-buster's son and that's what you'll always be.'

Hartford didn't flinch.

'Answer my question, Mr McGreggor.'

The fast drumming of hoofbeats sounded at the far end of the street. A lone rider approached at the gallop, a cloud of trail dust exploding behind him. The sheriff stepped down off his porch and shaded his eyes against the sun.

The rider jerked his horse to a standstill outside the saloon, leapt down from the saddle and threw the reins over the hitching rail. The sheriff shouted something and hobbled painfully across the street to try to catch up with him but he was too slow. The rider took the porch steps two at a time.

'Not now, Sheriff,' he shouted. 'I got to see Mary May.'

THIRTEEN

The sheriff pulled himself awkwardly up the saloon steps, his breath shortened to gasps of pain. His left hand grabbed the rail, his right clutched his .45. Hartford pushed in front of him and burst through the saloon doors. Inside, Boone had seized Mary May by the arm. Horrified townsfolk pressed themselves back against the walls. Chairs clattered over. Glasses smashed. On their feet, Logan and the boys from McGreggor's ranch eyed the distance to their gun belts hanging by the door. Pearl stood behind the bar holding her twelve-gauge just out of sight. Boone's gun was in his hand. He threatened the crowd with wide sweeping gestures and shouted about no one trying to stop him.

'You're coming with me.' He started to frogmarch Mary May towards the door. 'They're saying things about me. I got to talk to you.'

'Got to put your gun away, Boone.' Hartford stood square in the doorway, his Colt still in its holster. His words weren't loud or angry, not a command just a flat statement of fact.

Boone hesitated, seemed to recognize his brother for the first time, seemed to wonder what he was doing there. He glanced round the room and noticed the faces of McGreggor's hands, Pearl, Pops and Greely, the townsfolk, people he had known all his life. He was centre stage.

'I ain't going to marry you, Boone.' Mary May's voice cut through the commotion.

Boone turned to her, shock turned to relief in his face.

'That's what I came to tell you. Me and you married don't make sense at all. I just ain't the settling down type, Mary May.'

Still holding Mary May by the arm, he waved his gun at the men blocking the door.

'Now get the hell out of the way.'

'Can't do that, Boone.' It was the sheriff's voice. 'Just put your gun down.'

Colour drained from Boone's face. It was the same old sheriff who he delighted in running rings round as a kid, who hauled him home whenever he helped himself to candy from the store or broke someone's window with his catapult or put a frog in a girl's hair. It was as if he was ten years old again; it was almost funny. He looked round the room expecting people to see how funny this was. Everyone stared, poker faces set against him, just like when he got in trouble all those years ago. And he was always in trouble. The silence pressed on his ears. Why didn't anyone say anything? He waved his gun again. He was on his own like he always was. Mary May cried out as he tightened his grip on her arm.

'Out of my way.' He heard his own words echo inside his head. He clamped his fist tight, afraid Mary May was going to slip away like an eel. What was she struggling for? Hadn't he come here to do the right thing? To tell her face-to-face that he was too wild, too free to settle down. How could he be expected to waste his life breaking his back day after day on some miserable plot of dirt? Of course he was right, just look what had happened to his pa.

That was the moment Boone realized that the sheriff was holding a gun. The old fool. He had his .45 in his hand and the hammer was pulled back. No one else had drawn a gun. Hartford was right in front of him, he wasn't holding a gun. McGreggor was there, he was empty handed. It was only Sheriff Milton who still had it in for him, just like when he was a kid. The sheriff should be pleased he was here. He had come to do the right thing by Mary May in front of everyone, in front of the whole town. And this was the thanks the sheriff gave him. He hated him probably. And why? No reason for it.

Mary May was screaming now. Something about how he was breaking her arm. Her screams cut into his thoughts like blades, however much he tried to ignore them. Turned out she was just like all the rest of them, the sheriff, his clever brother, his ma's favourite, who had high-tailed it to Chicago and left him condemned to a sodbuster's life, all these people who hadn't got anything better to do than stare at him. He could feel their eyes on him, drilling into him.

Boone shook Mary May hard then to make her shut up, to let him think, but she only screamed louder. Then other people were shouting, all of them maybe. He could see their mouths moving, how twisted their faces were, his brother, McGreggor, the sheriff, all of them. But he couldn't make out their words. Mary May's screaming filled his head and so he shook her a third time. Hard. He had to make her stop. Had to. Or he couldn't think at all. Then he saw the sheriff wave his .45. The old fool. What did he think he was doing? With Mary May's screams slashing at his brain, Boone raised his gun and fired.

The shot sounded like someone had exploded a dynamite charge. The walls shook. Shouting erupted now, screams, men's voices, women's voices. At the same time, Mary May swung herself in front of him, made a grab for his gun with her other hand. She was yelling at him too, crying, he felt her hair brush across his face and smelled the scent of lavender.

Then someone pulled the floor away. He was on his back with Hartford kneeling on his chest. He had let go of Mary May, the sheriff was standing on his wrist and was shouting something about his gun. Hartford drew back his fist and slugged him. He heard his teeth crack, felt lightning strike inside his head. Then he felt his body relax as if he was about to float off somewhere. His limbs were light and loose and voices whirlpooled above him. He wasn't in the saloon anymore.

Yes he was. People were hauling him to his feet, holding him up while they dragged him across the floor, two of them, Hartford and the sheriff. His legs wouldn't work properly, his vision misted. In the distance he could hear Mary May crying. They sat him down on a chair. Someone tied his hands behind him. Why? he wondered. He was too weak to move anyway. His head swirled and he tasted blood in his mouth.

As Boone's head cleared, he heard them arguing about him. The sheriff's voice was hoarse with anger, Hartford's stern and cold. Annie was pleading with them and Pearl was saying something about guns in the saloon.

'Think you can walk in here and take a shot at me?' the sheriff snarled.

'Please, Sheriff, please.' Annie was sobbing, her words catching in her throat. 'You know what he's like. He didn't set out to do that . . .' Her voice trailed away.

They had sat Boone in the middle of the room where he had stood with Mary May a few minutes before. Everyone was gathered round him, their eyes hard, unforgiving. Over by the bar, Pearl had her arm around Mary May.

'Mary May's a brave girl.' The sheriff regained his sense of dignity. 'Knocking that gun aside saved my life. Nearly got herself shot in the process.'

Murmurs of agreement echoed in the crowd. Boone tried to catch Mary May's eye but she wouldn't look at him. He hung his head.

'She had the good sense to see there was no future with you too.' The sheriff couldn't resist turning the knife. 'You may think you broke with her, but she told us that was her intention before you turned up.'

Boone looked over towards Mary May again.

'This day may not have turned out how you all thought,' the sheriff addressed the crowd. 'But I had my suspicions and I've got a thing or two to say. There's a matter we've all got to face up to, something we've all got to deal with. Ordinarily, Credence is a peaceful place. But recently there's been cattle rustling, a guy busted out of jail and we've had a dead man at Snake's Creek.'

Silence fell on the room. Some of the crowd met the sheriff's stare, Jake Nudd inspected his boots, Logan stared at the ceiling, even McGreggor shifted uneasily. Hartford got ready to say his piece. He had seen evidence of rustling with his own eyes, whatever excuse McGreggor came up with.

'You had the wrong man, Sheriff.' At the back of the room, Jake Nudd got to his feet. His friends hissed at him to sit down but he ignored them. 'I ain't no rustler. I've worked all the ranches between here and Abilene one time or another. Mr McGreggor paid us to find his steers that had got mixed in with the Dunmore herd, that's all.'

'Without letting Mr Dunmore in on this little arrangement.' The sheriff's sarcasm made Nudd shift his weight from foot to foot. 'You were being paid to work on the Lazy D at the time, weren't you Jake?'

Everyone turned to stare at Jake. From the murmur of agreement, the sheriff judged the weight of opinion was behind him.

'Seems to me like you deserved a night in jail.'

Nudd inspected his boots again. He had polished them that morning expecting to attend a wedding party where everything would be forgiven and forgotten. Instead, here he was, on the spot.

'On top of that, the minute my back's turned your friends bust you out. Seems to me you all owe me a night in the lock-up.'

People were openly nodding agreement; it was clear the crowd was on the sheriff's side. Logan and the others pulled Jake Nudd down into his seat again and told him to shut his trap.

'Anyhow, I'll deal with you later,' the sheriff glared at them. 'That ain't the only rustling we've got going on.'

'You all know I'm a Pinkerton Agent.' Hartford took his cue.

'Sheriff's right. Mr Dunmore contacted our Chicago office to ask for help to track down rustlers. We had a wire this morning. The agent up in Abilene has uncovered a rustling operation which means steers are being moved north. We're waiting for more details. In the mean time my instructions are to place Boone Hartford under arrest.'

There were gasps from the crowd, whispers about brother arresting brother. Somewhere at the back of everyone, Annie sobbed. Boone lifted his head and stared, he looked defeated.

'Never had a construction job in Dallas, did you Boone?' Sheriff Milton said grimly. 'All that time you were away, you were arranging the drive north for longhorns cut from McGreggor's and the Lazy D herds. Probably other ranches as well.'

Boone didn't protest. He held the sheriff's gaze for a moment and then his eyes slid away.

The sheriff tucked his thumbs into his belt and prepared to move on. The set of his jaw said that he had figured things out and was about to do his job dispensing justice, come what may. Pain in his knees, which ordinarily would have prevented him from standing for so long, didn't seem to trouble him at all.

'Now we're getting on to the killing of Mr Charles Dunmore,' the sheriff announced. 'Pearl, why don't you take Miss Dunmore out on to the porch while I go through this?'

'No.' Mary May stood up, angry and determined in spite of her tears.

'I'm staying, Sheriff. You go right ahead and say what you're going to say.'

'Dunmore wasn't a popular man.' The sheriff avoided looking in Mary May's direction and pressed ahead. 'I heard complaints about him all over. Even you, Pops.' The sheriff turned his gaze to where Pops Wardell sat in the corner. His head was nodding and he looked as if he was just about to doze off.

'Me?' Pops was suddenly wide awake and trying to figure out whether or not he was being accused of something. 'All I said was he threw me out of Snake's

Creek.' Then it dawned on him that that was the exact spot where Dunmore's body had been found. 'Now just a minute, Sheriff, I've been fishing up there for years. Everyone knows that.'

'All right, Pops, no one's accusing you,' the sheriff assured him and shifted attention to Greely. 'I've heard you speak against him, Bill.'

'Only said he never left me a tip, that's all.' Greely hadn't expected to be dragged into this. 'What are you saying, Sheriff?'

The sheriff swung his gaze across the room to where Jake Nudd was trying to hide behind Logan and Clyde Shorter.

'Logan, what about you? Ever say you wanted Dunmore dead?'

'I just meant Dunmore accused us of stealing his beeves.' Logan pulled at the kerchief knotted at his throat.

'Dunmore complained to me, fired you and got your friend Jake tossed in jail,' the sheriff pressed him.

'They weren't his beeves; they were Mr McGreggor's.' Logan was on the back foot. A raspberry-coloured blush crept up his neck. 'Look, Sheriff, I never would have. . . .'

'And you, Clyde. Ever want Dunmore out of the way?' The sheriff turned to Clyde Shorter.

Shorter looked like a hooked fish. His eyes bulged and his mouth moved but no words came out.

'What about you, Jake?' The sheriff turned to where Jake Nudd was hunched down behind his friends, hoping the sheriff would forget about him. 'You were the one who spent the night in a cell. What kind of a grudge did you hold against Dunmore?'

Over by the bar, Mary May sobbed bitterly. Pearl tightened her arm round her shoulder and drew her close. People began to doubt that she was right to stay behind. The poor girl had just lost her father and to hear him talked about like this must be agonising. Sympathy for her was palpable.

'Mary May, now I've got something to ask you.' The sheriff's voice was gentle, understanding. 'You know I didn't intend you to hear all that. Just remember that every small town has its resentments, it's part of the woodwork.'

Mary May dabbed her eyes with a handkerchief.

'Everyone knows you had a falling out with your pa, Mary May.' The sheriff quietened his voice until it was barely above a whisper. 'And when you're young, things get out of hand. You were running around with Boone like some kind of wildness had gotten into you. We all saw it. No secret that your pa had no time for Boone. You defied him to his face, Mary May.' The sheriff paused.

Mary May had stopped crying now. White-faced, she pulled away from Pearl, sat up upright and let the sheriff lecture her. Horrified, people began to wonder which way the sheriff's questions were heading. They stared at Mary May. Beneath her tears and display of grief, was this wilful girl capable of turning on her own kin?

In the saloon, silence fell. Mary May stared at the

sheriff, hurt and anger in her face, her eyes as hard as bullets. The memory of all the times she had been criticised, lectured, reprimanded, punished by her father was in her now. She was hearing again all his harsh words which had cut her so deeply and which he had assured her over and over were for her own good. The sheriff was standing in front of her, accusing her just like her pa used to do. It was as if her father had returned from the grave.

'Did you follow your pa out to Snake's Creek two days ago?' The sheriff's voice was still gentle and his gaze was fixed on her. 'Did you shoot him, Mary May?'

The question hung in the air. The townspeople looked from one to the other. Had they heard right? Pops turned to Bill Greely, Pearl looked to Hartford, Logan and Shorter were open-mouthed. They all stared at Mary May's wan, tearstained face. They saw how she sat straight-backed and looked the sheriff in the eye. They saw her expression of hurt and defiance and how her hands twisted her handkerchief until it was rope. Could Mary May have killed her own father?

'I did it.'

It was Boone's voice. He turned to Mary May for a second and his look contained a message. Everyone saw it but only she understood what it was. Then he turned and faced the sheriff. His hair was untidy, his face was bruised and there was blood on his lip.

'I shot Dunmore out at Snake's Creek.'

A breeze must have picked up somewhere, sand

sifted in under the saloon door, and dust motes spun in the lines of sunlight. Silence weighed down on the room. No one moved. No one spoke.

Aware that everyone was watching him, Boone lifted his head to meet the sheriff's gaze. He had been the focus of the town's attention often enough, but never like this. He had always been in the wrong, caught out, accused of something. As his notoriety grew, people shunned him and kept away. No one liked him, he knew it. He told himself that he was too big for this small town. He was made for a hard-riding, daredevil life, excitement and fun. If that meant he came into conflict with his pa, with the sheriff, with his neighbours, well, that was part of it. No one was going to hold him down.

Then Boone found Mary May. The quiet, awkward girl he had known as a kid had turned into this beautiful young woman. Like him, she felt stifled by her pa and the dull routine of daily life. Like him, she wanted a taste of freedom. She would sneak out of her house to go on midnight rides with him; she would disobey her pa and meet him down by the Blue River where they would talk until sundown. She encouraged him to quit the farm for no other reason than that she knew it was what he wanted.

As far as Boone was concerned, there was no one else like Mary May. So one day, which happened to be a day she had argued with her pa worse than usual, he asked her to marry him. Amidst laughter and disbelief at her own daring, she said yes.

Boone looked up. There was old Sheriff Milton

hissing at Mary May like a snake, standing there accusing Mary May in the same soft-voiced, whispering way he used to accuse him of stealing candy from the store when he was a kid. Boone used to wish the sheriff would yell at him, show that he was angry. It made his blood boil so badly, he used to shout out not caring who knew that he was guilty. No matter. Right now, he was taking the fall for his girl in front of everybody. What could he do that was better than that?

'I did it, Sheriff,' Boone said again.

'How?'

The question surprised him. But then he should have guessed the sheriff would try to trick him. Boone looked at the watching faces. Did they appreciate how fine his course of action was, how courageous, how noble?

'Scattergun.' Boone wasn't going to fall for anything. He answered the question loud and clear so there could be no mistake.

'In the back?' The sheriff spoke so quietly, you had to strain to hear him.

Now, this was a trick. This was the sheriff trying to make him look bad. Here he was doing something right and the sheriff was painting it so he looked like a coward.

Boone kept hold of his temper.

'He called me out, then he lost his nerve, turned to run just as I fired.' Turned out it wasn't so hard to out-manoeuvre old Sheriff Milton after all.

There was a gasp then. A woman somewhere in

the crowd stifled a scream. People shifted in their seats. There were mutterings in the crowd. As the horror of this confession hit home, people stared at Boone with contempt. Suddenly his lofty gesture, doing the right thing, coming clean and protecting Mary May seemed an ugly pantomime.

'In that case,' the sheriff said quickly. 'I'm putting you under arrest and charging you with the shooting of Charles Dunmore. I'll take you to jail in Abilene myself and next time a hanging judge passes through, I'll make sure you stand trial. Your confession will be evidence and the people in this room will be witnesses.'

'He's lying, Sheriff.' It was a woman's voice from the back of the crowd. 'He made all that up to protect his girl.'

Boone recognized the voice. At least one person understood how chivalrous he was. It was his sister, Annie.

'You got something to tell us all, Annie?' the sheriff prompted. 'You know something?'

'My pa shot Dunmore,' Annie said.

Whispers spread through the onlookers like a breeze through dry leaves. Some people shook their heads in disbelief; others stared in horror.

'I took him out to Snake's Creek in the buggy,' Annie continued. 'He used to love fishing out there. Mr Dunmore rode up and ordered us off his land. There was an argument. He said pa should know that Boone was nowhere near good enough for Mary May. Boone would never have her because he aimed

147

to make sure of it.' Annie had started confidently, but now she was trembling and struggled to get her words out. 'Then he said Pa hadn't got long to go and if he wouldn't sell him the farm, he'd take it anyway after he was dead. Boone wouldn't have it and nor would I.'

As if she had run out of strength, Annie stopped talking. She stared at her hands in her lap and avoided everyone's gaze.

'Now, Annie,' the sheriff began softly. 'I know you want to protect your brother, that's only natural. Just think carefully about what you're saying.'

'It's the truth, Sheriff,' Annie said simply.

Hartford walked round the back of the crowd and put his arm round Annie's shoulders. She looked as frail as a bird.

'Boone has confessed,' the sheriff said. 'Everyone heard it. He had the opportunity; he could have followed Dunmore out to Snake's Creek. He had the motive; Dunmore had forbidden him to carry on with Mary May. His blood was up, they'd had a fight that afternoon. Everyone knows they hated each other.'

'If you don't believe me, Sheriff, I got a witness.' Annie stood up and pushed Hartford away. 'It wasn't just me who saw the shooting.'

'Witness?' The sheriff almost laughed. 'You'd make up anything to protect your brother, wouldn't you?'

'I'm the witness, Sheriff.' Pops Wardell clambered to his feet. 'I was at the creek when Annie brought her pa out there in the buggy. Joe was mighty sick, Sheriff. Known him a long time, broke my heart to see him like that.'

Pops Wardell's old shoulders dropped, it was as if he had slung a heavy pack on his back.

'Dunmore came along, started ordering me off his land. Going on about how this wasn't the first time and what he'd do if I came out there again.' Pops looked across at Annie and smiled at her. 'When he saw Joe Hartford, he started mocking him, asking what was a sick old man doing out here. Said it wouldn't be long before Joe was gone and how he'd annexe his farm before his body was cold.'

Pops Wardell paused. He didn't take his eyes off Annie.

'Joe reached into the back of the buggy, picked up his scattergun and opened both barrels. Next second Dunmore dropped as dead as a stone.'

'Shot him face to face while Dunmore was still arguing with him?' The sheriff had to be certain.

'Would have, if he could have got to his scattergun quick enough,' Pops looked straight into the sheriff's eyes. 'Took him a moment, so Dunmore had turned away by then. Joe Hartford shot him in the back.'

FOURTEEN

Back in his office, another wire from the commanding officer at Fort Worth was waiting for the sheriff. An army patrol had come across a gang cutting a herd on the Territory border with the intention of driving the longhorns across country to join the Western Trail to Dodge.

At first, the gang claimed to be free grazers on some itinerant journey across north Texas, but their cover story soon fell apart and it didn't take the commander long to realize that the cowboys his men had picked up weren't capable of running an operation like this by themselves. There had to be someone behind it to let them know when a herd would be coming through, arrange supplies and coordinate with a buyer at the other end. Faced with the prospect of army justice, the gang quickly admitted that the man they were working for was called Boone Hartford from a little town called Credence, a day's ride north of Dallas.

'Dunmore's instincts were right.' The sheriff

handed the wire to Hartford. 'His herd was being cut and Boone was a bad apple. He just never put the two together.'

In the cell that adjoined the office, Boone hung his head.

Hartford remembered his pa on the porch of the farmhouse, ill and angry, with the row between Boone and Dunmore going on inside and Mary May crying. He remembered his pa's scattergun and his fishing pole propped up beside his chair and Mary May talking about how more than anything he loved to be taken on buggy rides.

When Hartford and the sheriff rode out to the creek to inspect the place where Dunmore died, he'd noticed wheel tracks in the dirt. '*Bill Greely bring a wagon out here when he came to pick up the body?*'

'*No sir,' Pops said. 'I wanted him to but he wouldn't do it. Said he wouldn't be able to get it close enough to the river. Brought a mule out from the stable, carried the body back to town on that.*' Pops' face hadn't given anything away.

Annie had told the truth.

By the time Hartford got back to the saloon, most of the bunting had been taken down. Pops Wardell was holding a ladder for Greely while Pearl supervised.

Logan came up to him, solemn-faced. Clyde Shorter and Jake Nudd stood behind him and let him do the talking.

'Sheriff over in his office?'

What was this about? Like everyone else, Logan had seen the sheriff cross the street.

'Sheriff's a good man. Everyone knows that.' Logan cleared his throat, trying to muster his words. 'Me and Clyde just wanted to apologise. We shouldn't have busted Jake out of jail like that. We were just mad with the sheriff for taking Dunmore's side. . . .' His words petered out as he found himself being critical of a dead man.

'Better head over to his office and tell him, Logan.' Hartford made it easy for him. 'He'll appreciate that.'

The last of the bunting lay in a heap in the middle of the saloon floor. McGreggor sat at a corner table with Charlie Nudd, a bottle of Pearl's red eye between them. The men clinked glasses, clearly coming to an agreement about something. Annie and Mary May were keeping themselves busy folding up the bunting. The women worked quickly together, catching each other's eye, smiling and finding relief in doing this simple task together. Pearl was behind the bar. Just as Pops and Greely manoeuvred the ladder ready to take it back to the livery, the sheriff pushed open the saloon door, followed by Logan and his boys.

'Now listen up,' the sheriff called for attention and waited while Pops and Greely put down the ladder. 'A few things I've got to say.'

Grave-faced, he relayed the news of the wire from Fort Worth. Mary May helped Annie towards a chair, stood behind her and laid a comforting hand on her shoulder. All the time the sheriff was speaking, Annie didn't take her eyes off Hartford.

'Boone will stand trial and if he's found guilty, he'll have to pay for his crime under the law,' the sheriff said.

'Will they hang him, Sheriff?' Annie sounded afraid.

'In the old days they would have,' the sheriff said. 'But Dunmore ain't around to press charges. It will be Boone's word against the fellas they caught red-handed.'

'I got something to say, Sheriff.' Used to taking charge, McGreggor spoke up. 'I've been talking to Charlie here and he'd be happy to ride over and help to run the Hartford farm for the time being. Charlie and I reckon you could do with some help, Miss Annie.'

McGreggor carried on quickly without giving Annie time to reply.

'As far as the Lazy D goes. I'll make you a fair offer, when you're ready, Mary May. In the meantime, you can come and live at the McGreggor house. The Lazy D is a big place, it could get mighty lonely out there.'

McGreggor looked pleased with himself. As self-appointed benefactor, he felt he had done well. To everyone else though, his offers of help sounded like orders.

'I ain't finished,' the sheriff said testily – McGreggor had stolen his thunder. 'Truth is, what with my knees and all, I'm intending to retire. Now this rustling business is cleared up, it seems about as good a time as any.' He looked at the familiar faces round the room. Annie and Mary May smiled fondly.

Pearl leaned on the bar. McGreggor and Charlie raised their glasses. Even Logan looked mildly disappointed.

'Thing is, I've got to find a replacement. This town doesn't require a full time sheriff now. It needs someone who knows the place, someone trustworthy for folks to turn to. That's why I'm going to ask Hart if he'll take it on.'

Hartford was stunned. Everyone was looking at him. Annie was smiling.

'You sure sprung this on me, Sheriff.' Hartford felt pride rise up in him, a sudden warmth as if he had stood next to a stove. 'I'll have to think about this. The Agency is waiting for my report about the rustling. But thank you.'

'While you're thinking, I'm taking the step of appointing Pearl as the new deputy,' the sheriff went on. 'She can cover for you until you make up your mind.'

Pearl whooped with surprise and delight.

'Thank you, Sheriff. Mighty nice of you.'

'Just for the record.' The sheriff looked at McGreggor. 'Anyone who can make a bunch of hard-boiled cowhands leave their guns at the door every time they enter a saloon is more than fit to be a deputy in this town.'

Mary May had been whispering to Annie while all this had been going on.

'Mr McGreggor,' she said. 'You're making me a kind offer, but I'll be living at the farm with Annie for a while. Maybe we could call on Charlie when we need him but if he's willing, I'd like him to take over at the Lazy D for the short term. We can discuss bringing the two ranches together in a few weeks maybe.'

McGreggor eyed her with a new respect. This was no longer the distraught girl who had thrown herself on his mercy when she discovered what happened to her father. Gently, politely and firmly, she had stood up to him. She treated him like a partner in business, offered courtesy and demanded the same.

Charlie Nudd beamed. 'I can ride between the farm and the Lazy D, no problem.'

'It's a deal, then.' McGreggor raised his glass.

The sheriff was assuming he'd say yes, Hartford thought. By itself, the offer of becoming sheriff of Credence wasn't something he'd ever wished for. But the farm needed more work than Charlie could do in the short term and would probably be too much for Annie, even with Mary May's help. The offer of the sheriff's job was one more reason why he should come home.

The following day, rain came as a shock. It had been dry for weeks, pale skies, clouds as thin as feathers and concussing heat. The miles of buffalo grass prairie that stretched south of the town were brown and parched and no one had ever known the level of the Blue River so low. But early in the morning, a wind got up, teased the dust from the town street and tossed it in the air. A warm south wind at this time of year was advance warning of a tornado. Before they

left for Dunmore's funeral at the Lazy D, the townsfolk made sure nothing was left lying around in their
yards, bolted their doors and windows and took their
horses up to Greely's livery.

Dunmore's grave had been dug on a rise which
overlooked the ranch house and the southern
portion of Lazy D land. The whole town and all the
ranch hands were there, even Boone, handcuffed
and standing beside the sheriff at the back of the
crowd. There was dampness in the air which made
the preacher hurry. He spoke respectfully about how
the achievements of Dunmore's life were all around
them, his fine ranch house, his land and his cattle.
He praised Mary May for her fortitude and insisted
that no man could want for a more loyal or loving
daughter. Supported on one side by McGreggor and
on the other by Annie, Mary May sobbed as the
ranch hands lowered the pine coffin. Away to the
south, dark clouds built on the horizon and everyone
checked the sky.

From the Lazy D, the crowd then moved to the
Hartford farm. In a corner of the pasture behind the
house, beside his wife's grave, McGreggor's men
lowered Joe Hartford's coffin into the ground. As
Hart, Boone and Annie stepped forward to cast
handfuls of dirt into the grave, a fine warm rain
started to fall. It was like gauze, soft and comforting.
It caressed the faces of anyone who looked up and
the wind which carried it was gentle and warm.
Charlie Nudd handed round shovels and made sure
the men worked quickly.

156

Annie led the way inside, where she had set jugs of Joe Hartford's potato wine on the kitchen table. The sheriff let Boone stay for a while but no one seemed interested in talking to him. Annie was busy with the food and Hartford stayed outside on the porch. After half an hour, Boone had had enough and asked the sheriff to take him back to jail. It wasn't long before people began to make their excuses, concerned to slip away before the weather broke. The rain had left off for a while but the wind had picked up and inky clouds scudded in front of the sun. Worried that his herd would be spooked by the coming storm, McGreggor ordered his men back to the ranch. Charlie Nudd offered to stay, but Annie turned him down. The preacher took Pearl, Pops and Bill Greely back to town in his wagon. Mary May insisted on staying with Annie.

Taking care not to sit in his pa's old rocking chair, Hartford found a seat on the porch and sat down with Annie and Mary May to watch the weather blow in.

'I'm turning down the sheriff's offer,' he said. 'I'll stay for a couple of weeks as there are some jobs need doing around here.'

'Still going to be a Pinkerton?' Annie smiled at him. 'I'm glad, Hart. It's what you always wanted.'

'I'll get back as often as I can,' Hartford said quickly, he had expected Annie to be disappointed. 'See you, help out on the farm.'

'I think we should sell the farm to McGreggor,' Annie said quietly. 'You've got your life, now I want mine.'

'That's what I'm going to do,' Mary may cut in. 'McGreggor wants to buy the Lazy D. I know he'll take the farm as well.'

Hartford saw the excitement in both women's faces.

'When McGreggor buys the Lazy D, I'm going to have a house built right in the centre of Dallas.' Mary May could hardly contain herself. 'It will be a fine brick house with beautiful windows, a view over the street and a garden with a plane tree where people can come calling and I can take tea in the afternoons. I've asked Annie to come and live there with me.'

'That's what I want to do. Mary May says I can live there for nothing, but I've told her I'll get a job and pay my way. I'm so excited, Hart.'

'A job?' Hartford didn't know what to say.

'Teaching little children. They say the railroad will reach Dallas inside two years. The workers will bring their families. I could teach the children their letters. I could do it in a room in Mary May's house and pay her rent for it.'

'A school?' Hartford could see the joy in his sister's face. 'What about Credence, won't you miss it?'

'Credence is done, Hart. Anyone can see that. With Sheriff Milton retired, there won't be a town. Pearl says the sheriff thinks the town can go on the way it always has. But it can't. She doesn't want to be a deputy here any more than you want to be sheriff. She plans to hand over the saloon to Bill Greely and Pops and open a joint in Dallas. If they don't want to take it on, she says they can come to Dallas with her. Reckons she'll start with a tent down where they'll be building the railroad and when she's made enough money, she'll open a place in town.'

Away on the southern horizon lightning forked into the ground and a minute later, thunder rolled across the distant sky. The air pressure slackened, the wind gathered and a veil of warm rain gusted across the yard in front of them. Sheltered by the porch roof, they sat back. The rain refreshed the land and the wind brought a coolness they had not felt for weeks. Almost in front of their eyes, green shoots appeared amongst the parched grass.